INITIATED

MAYA DANIELS

UNTAMED

MAYA DANIELS

VIRGIL
BOOKS

By Maya Daniels

Daywalker Series

Investigated

Infiltrated

Instigated

Initiated

Infuriated

Ignited

Vinci Books

vinci-books.com

Published by Vinci Books Ltd in 2026

1

A CIP catalogue record for this book is available from the British Library.

Paperback ISBN: 9781036706753

The EU GPSR authorised representative is Logos Europe, 9 rue Nicolas Poussion, 17000 La Rochelle, France
contact@logoseurope.eu

Chapter One

"You have got to be kidding me!"

Snarling, my fangs drop from the freaking chaos in front of my eyes. Zoltan shoves me behind his back the second we step out of the portal, both of us ducking to avoid the blast of magic hurling through the air aimed at our heads. The wards of the portal prevent whatever spell is thrown from damaging our gateway to the human world sending sparks all over the place like some creepy fireworks show, burning like hell when it lands on my exposed skin. The frustrated growl coming out of Zoltan tells me he is not doing much better than me.

"What in the fates name is going on?"

My words come out shaky while I run to the line of trees in a half crouch, Zoltan yanking on my arm as he guides us there. From what I was able to see before my eyes bulged out of my skull, everyone in the academy is in the clearing surrounding the portal. You can't tell who is fighting whom, growls, snarls, and roars creating a constant hum around my head making me feel dizzy. The air is saturated with magic, tightening my skin while forcing my own power to swirl and pulse at the center of my chest. The only thing keeping me from losing my shit is the lack of white clothing that indicates hunters are in the middle of this clusterfuck.

A wolf comes out of the forest, snapping his head my way as he sails through the trees. He barely misses us. I jerk back and twist around, pulling Zoltan along with me at the last moment. The shifter lands gracefully on the ground but doesn't leave to join the fight like I expect him to. He also doesn't attack. The moon shines on his fur like liquid steel when he hunches down baring his sharp canines. Lifting his muzzle at the sky, he howls, and the sound raises goosebumps all over my arms and legs. It's a call, I just don't know what kind. Is it to announce his presence, to let his brethren know he's arrived? Or is it to tell them where we are? If it's the latter, Zoltan and I are about to fight for our lives … again. I see the vampire tucking the damn book he was holding at the small of his back, covering it with his shirt.

Answering calls echo through the night, and the short hairs on the back of my neck stand at attention when a deep growl followed by a hissing purr reaches my ears. Glancing up, I can't miss the panther poised on top of a thick branch above our heads, his legs bent as if ready to pounce. The quickening of my heartbeat is not lost on the feline, or on Zoltan. I clench my jaw but don't feel too bad about freaking out since the noise the panther makes is the same one a person may hear a second before their throat is ripped out. Sharp pain zips through my neck and shoulders. My head jerks up and I lock gazes with the predator. Green eyes like jewels glitter in the pinpricks of the moonlight, the large black body blending into the shadows like a ghost. My heart wrenches to the back of my throat and lodges there for a moment before I realize the shifter is not looking at me. His entire focus is aimed over our heads at the fighting that hasn't paused for a second with our arrival.

"What the fuck is happening here?" Zoltan's deep voice makes me jump out of my skin.

Being just inside the line of trees, the shadows give us enough cover not to be noticed. I watch the wolf step back to where we are standing, his eyes never leaving the battle. The panther drops next to me with barely a sound, nudging me further into the forest with his massive body. I'm clutching Zoltan's hand for dear life while my mind short-circuits, unable to form a coherent thought even if my life depends on it. Thank God it doesn't. The hoots of owls spread over our heads and mix with the cacophony of flesh hitting flesh. A grunt sends a crackle of magic rippling through our surroundings and the wolf transforms in front of our eyes. Rolling his neck with a loud crack, he lifts from his crouch, taking his full human form once more.

"The Board riled everyone that didn't join us in the human realm, feeding them stories that we are deflecting from the cause since we are following Drake. They were waiting for us when we got back." The snarl of his animal is clear in his growled words. "Leo made us walk through the portal in large groups, so thankfully we lost only a few before we could fight back."

"Who is feeding the Board these bullshit stories?" Relieved that we don't have to fight these two, I snatch his arm and make him to look at me. "Roberti and Alexius are here?"

"Drake." He thumps his fist over his heart, and mine stutters against my ribcage. "The Board was waiting, calling us traitors. I don't know if someone filled their heads with it,

3

or if they did it on their own." His gray eyes turn on Zoltan and something passes between the two males—something that pisses me off.

"I see." The one word wonder is back and I glare at him.

"Oh, great!" I clap my hands like a two-year-old. "Good for you, bloodsucker. I, on the other hand, don't see shit." Zoltan's lips twitch and I want to slap the smirk off his pretty face. "Want to share?"

"You are a bloodsucker, too." Zoltan's blue eyes darken, the smoldering gaze reminding me of what happened in the shower not that long ago. Butterflies erupt in my lower belly, making me squirm.

"Half ..." Sounding breathless, I can't hide the damn reaction my body has to him.

His nostrils flare.

"The Board has the vampires and a good number of others on their side." The shifter clears his throat angling his body away from me to hide the jutting erection between his thighs.

Oh, great. Thanks to the jerk gloating at me, I'm throwing fuck me vibes like there is no tomorrow, at least if his growing smile is any indication. *Perfect timing Franky, like always.* My inner voice couldn't sound snarkier if it tried.

"All the vampires are backing them up?" Zoltan's voice is low and he doesn't take his eyes off me. A muscle jumps in his jaw.

"Not all. After Astara came through a good chunk have our back. Silas's son and his lackeys are still fighting and will never stray from what that old fool says." With great difficulty, I look away from the vamp just as the shifter frowns, his head tilting to the side as if he is trying to hear something. "Perfect, Leo is coming this way. I'll go help the others out."

With a sharp nod at Zoltan and another thump of his fist over his heart aimed at me, he shifts and bolts out of the trees. I hiss, startled when something brushes against my arm. The panther nudges me to the side and shoves his head under my hand. I forget the large cat is here and I have a predator as silent as death standing next to me. *This is why you'll die one of these days, for not paying attention.* The voice in my head reminds me of my shortcomings.

"Is this another of the plans you made without letting the rest of us know?" I round on Zoltan, and if I sound bitter, it's because I am.

I still haven't forgiven him for planning to be captured and giving that asshole Roberti the pleasure of turning him feral. The jerk can act tough and like he is invincible as much as he likes, but it doesn't change anything. He didn't know my blood could cure him. None of us knew, and if it wasn't for Myst—regardless how lacking her tactics were— we would've lost him. One of us would've had to kill him. The sight of Zoltan's red eyes burning with bloodlust and his beautiful face twisted in a snarl is seared into my retinas for eternity. My blood curdles just thinking about it. Seeing him flinch like I slapped him soothes me, but only just. Definitely not enough.

"I knew nothing of this …" Zoltan's long fingers press on his forehead, rubbing it harshly as if trying to relieve a headache. "I suspected it might come down to it, I just hoped I was wrong."

Waving a hand in his face, I prompt him to keep talking, the fingers of my other hand scratching under the panther's jaw with a mind of their own. My insides vibrate from the deep, satisfied purr coming out of the shifter, who body checks me when I snatch my hand back. The panther's upper lip twitches into a snarl, his long teeth gleaming in the moonlight when the head twice the size of mine tilts up to display the displeasure. A line forms between Zoltan's brows and a thoughtful look crosses his face.

"Well?" Ignoring the jitters coursing through me, I shove the panther's head away and rub under his deadly jaw again. "What does that mean, Zoltan? I'm not planning to hide here like some sissy while they're trying to kill each other out there. Fighting the hunters is enough to keep all of us busy for a while without being at each other's throats."

"Those that were fighting by your side in the human world want to follow you, Francesca. You! Not the old simpletons that can't see anything other than their own noses." His eyes stay on the shifter for another long moment before turning his blue gaze on me. My lungs feel tight like there isn't enough air to inflate them when he says my name with that slightly unidentifiable accent of his. "The Board is not known to willingly share the power they have over everyone. You can't tell me it didn't cross your mind. You are too cunning not to have thought of it before."

Hell yes, I've thought of it. It's been drilling holes in my head since the night Roberti sent me into the gaping mouth of the hungry beast that is Daywalker Academy. I just stupidly thought that with the hunters almost decimating us twice that the old fools were more worried about keeping us alive. Keeping us still a secret to the humans, that should've made them more worried instead of how much influence they have over the rest of us. That pink tutu I threatened Soren with sounds more and more like a great possibility. He could've warned me if nothing else. A throbbing heartbeat starts at my temples, numbing my head.

"I wouldn't say cunning." Grinding my teeth, my nails

dig harder under the panther's chin and the asshole snaps his sharp jaw at me until I flinch away. "I'd say prepared so I can keep my head on my shoulders. Those like me need to have eyes in the back of our heads if we want to continue breathing. That's survival 101 in Sienna for you, pure blood. Not cunning." He narrows his eyes at me when I smile, more of a baring of teeth than anything else. I'm learning tricks from the shifter purring next to me real fast. "You and Fenrir on the other hand ..." My shoulder jerks up in a shrug. "Can you say the same?"

"They can't."

Leo steps out from between two trees, luckily with sweats hanging low on his hips. His hair is sticking out every which way in tufts, five slashes are rapidly healing on the right side of his torso, and his left arm is twitching from the residual magic still sizzling on it where he's been hit by a spell.

"None of us can say that. That's why they want to follow you, Drake. You are not power hungry, and that's refreshing." A confused look flashes through Leo's green eyes when he looks at the panther glued to my side, but it's so fast I would've missed it if I wasn't staring at him. "Zoltan." He nods at the now-glaring vamp.

"How many did we lose?" Zoltan is all business now, whatever is bothering him now pushed aside, though I have no doubt I'll hear all about it later.

"None." Leo rubs the back of his neck, his eyebrows disappearing in his hairline. "They are not trying to kill us, just incapacitating before we get dragged to the lower levels." His cheeks puff out when he blows a deep breath. "I'm thinking someone has been feeding the Board bullshit and they are not sure who to believe. It's the only reason we are not getting maimed and killed. Unless ..."

Him and Zoltan stare at each other, the sound of the fighting filling the space around us. Even the panther bristles along with me at the two males. All these unspoken, or half spoken things are fraying my nerves. More secrets, more puzzles and riddles that have proven to bring death and nothing else. The same shit Soren has been pulling since the day I met him.

I'm tired of it all.

"You three stay here. I'll be right back." I try to sidestep the panther, but the shifter only moves with me, as graceful as a dancer who is preventing me from leaving the cover of the trees. "Do you mind?"

Scowling at the damn animal, I knee it in the rump. His long tail flicks around, slapping my thigh like a whip. Yelping, I jump away from it when it comes the second time. Zoltan's feral growl causes the panther to crouch low, placing its long muscular body between me and the vamp as if the shifter is trying to protect me from him. My eyes dart around while I try to figure out how to best fight the cat if it attacks Zoltan. I freeze when I see Leo standing without worry and scratching his head in confusion.

"Don't just stand there." I snap at the wolf shifter. "What the fuck is wrong with this one? Is he going to attack?"

"If I didn't see him standing next to you while you were scratching him like a house pet a second ago, I would've said yes." The panther hisses at Leo menacingly, and my heart skips a beat from the sound. "But he is not joining the fight so he can protect you."

"Of course, he wants to protect me since he is a male." I hip check the damn cat out of my way. "I'm going to help the others. You can hide here until it's all clear."

I only manage to move about a couple of feet before a

heavy weight slams between my shoulders and pitches me forward. With just enough time to protect my face, my arms take the brunt of the impact when I faceplant on the forest floor. All the air exits my lungs with a loud oomph, twigs and sharp rocks digging into my skin. Hot air puffs the tiny hairs on the side of my face when the panther lowers those deadly teeth too close for comfort. His entire body is stretched on top of mine and leaves me gasping for air.

"I'd say he made his point." Zoltan sounds too amused and I vow silently that he is going to pay for this.

"It's not smart to go out there, Drake." Leo's bare feet come in my line of sight before he lowers on his haunches to peer down at me. "The Board is asking us to hand you over if we want them to stop attacking."

"Lovely," I gasp out, still fighting for air.

"They'll have to go through me first." My whole body turns cold at the promise of pain in Zoltan's voice.

Chapter Two

My cough only makes Zoltan audibly grind his teeth and clench his fists harder, his knuckles turning white. It does nothing to cover the choking laughter bubbling in my chest. Leo's constant snorting while he does his best to keep himself in check is not helping matters, either. Even the panther glares at me, those glittering eyes turned into slits while we dodge magic, claws, and snapping jaws through the clustered bodies fighting around us. If they think over two-hundred pounds of cat sitting on top of me can stop me from coming to help, they know better now.

The panther growls deep in his chest, his left ear flicking.

The same ear I twisted in my grip when I pinned him on the ground after wrestling for the longest two minutes of my life. The damn shifter is all muscle, and I'm lucky he gives up fast since he doesn't want to hurt me. There is no doubt in my mind that those sharp jaws would be feasting on my flesh if he was not on my side. His green gaze narrows further like he knows what I'm thinking, and I swallow thickly. *Don't provoke the grumpy cat, Franky,* I chide myself, bending back and going almost horizontal when a steam of bright orange magic zips in front of my face an inch from my nose.

"Well, this looks like fun." Huffing, I follow behind Zoltan, the panther sticking to my side and Leo taking the back. I have to compromise if I want out of that forest without fighting all three of them. "Never a dull moment. Keeps you on your toes." I continue blabbing to cover the nerves that are wracking chaos inside me.

Zoltan grunts.

We are back to Neanderthal times, where not even one-word answers or comments are necessary. I might be an ass for being stubborn, especially after everything that happened in the last day or two, but I can't in good conscience wait things out while others are being hurt because of me. If Zoltan can't understand that, I have misjudged his character and there is nothing left for us to discuss. I cringe when his fist connects to a vampire's jaw, snapping his neck in the process. The body drops like a rock at his feet but Zoltan plows on, his anger a palpable thing between us. Am I so naïve that I believe he cares about others as much as I do? Is he only protective and considerate of me because of what I am? Does he not care if anyone else lives or dies? Or maybe this is a power play of his own making, one he has been weaving like a cobweb while we are all focused elsewhere?

Uncertainty is like a fist shoved down my throat, and it chokes me.

Rubbing my knuckles between my breasts does nothing to stop the hot poker stabbing that spot relentlessly. If only it is physical, then I can pull it out and it will heal in no time. But with everyone hell bent to get their hands on me, all my fears are rising to the surface. It's making me paranoid, and that's the last thing I need so I do my best to push it away.

"I'll try sneaking up on Silas." Zoltan's baritone rasp snaps me out of the dark path my thoughts have wandered down. "He will stop this insanity when I have my hands around his neck. I would bet my life that this is his doing."

He leads us to where I can see Astara and Fenrir facing off against the three Board members, the Fae standing in front of them with his arms crossed over his chest while he looks down his nose at them all. My friend, on the other hand, is waving her arms animatedly, her eyes blazing in rage while screaming in their face. The three old idiots with their triumphant expressions are enjoying this more than any sane person should. Screams of pain and anger pierce the night, all due to their idiotic plans or quest for power. As expected, Soren is nowhere to be seen. Not even this gets his ass up.

"Tutu." Clenching my jaw hard enough to crack a tooth, I snarl under my breath. "With a shit ton of glitter."

"What?" Leo glances at me like I'm the one that has lost her mind.

"Nothing." Stomping next to Zoltan, I try to find the best way to go behind the old jerks. "Should I come with you or am I the distraction?" So far, no one has noticed we are forging a path between them. Everyone's focus, instead, is on not ending up with a severed limb or a broken neck.

A thrill flutters through me when Zoltan trains his gaze my way. A smile deadlier than any weapon pulls his lips up, but it doesn't reach his eyes. My skin pebbles when his power expands from his skin like a blast of air, the hairs escaping my braid blowing away from my face. The panther presses his body closer to my thigh, his purr as scary as Zoltan looks right now.

"Distraction." The gravel in that word sounds harsher when his fangs poke out under his upper lip. "I only need a second." Tilting his chin up at Leo and flicking a quick glance at the cat next to me, he disappears through the fighting bodies.

"Don't be a hero, Drake." Leo bumps his shoulder against mine when he steps next to me. "Zoltan knows them better than anyone. He knows what he is doing. Let's just get their attention, shall we?"

When I turn to him, he is out of his sweats and naked as the day he was born. "You planning on getting their attention by waving your cock in their face?" I swear the panther snickers, or maybe I'm going nuts.

"I'll have you know it is a legendary cock." He grins wolfishly at me. "Too bad you picked the vamp, Drake. You'll never know its glory." I'm unable to hold in my giggle when he puffs his chest out.

"I haven't picked anyone, mutt. But keep your fleas to yourself, yeah?"

"Mhm." His green gaze flicks to my neck and my hand jerks up, fingers pressing where Zoltan had his fangs in my neck a few hours ago. The knowing look on Leo's face makes me want to punch him in the nose.

"I have your back, just don't get too close to them." Not waiting on whatever I was going to say all humor drains from him and he shifts.

"Right." Blowing out a long breath, I roll my shoulders. "Zoltan gets to have all the fun while I play Doctor Doolittle here." Snickering at the matching growls from the two shifters, I inch to the side to get a better look. "Okay boys …"

A blood curdling cry comes out of the panther and drowns my words. The deep purr that follows is so deep the ground under my feet vibrates from it. It silences the sounds that were creating the constant buzz in the air around us. Hundreds of eyes turn in my direction, the weight of the stares rooting me in place. Leo's wolf howls, the call more of a war cry than anything else. It snaps everyone back into action and I find myself surrounded by people. At first my knees bend slightly because I'm preparing to fight my way through them, at least until I realize they are forming a circle around me.

I glare at the wolf and the panther.

"I don't need to be protected." Grinding the words out, I march ahead and everyone else moves fluidly right beside me. "This is fucking ridiculous!"

Like I haven't spoken at all, they ignore me, the two shifters trotting on either side of me without a care in the world. Well Leo is trotting, his tail wagging just to piss me off I'm sure. The panther prowls and each press of his plate-sized paw on the ground is calculated and deadly as if he's daring someone to step in his path. His black coat is reflecting the moon like an oil spill with each move of his powerful legs. Some of the vampires, along with a demon or two, try to push through the protective shield formed around me but give up pretty fast when my self-appointed protectors get more vicious.

"Hey assholes!" All three Board members jerk their heads my way at the shout. "Here I am." Spreading my arms wide, I let my fangs drop when I grin at them. "Francesca Drake at your service." Executing a perfect bow, I flick my braid that fell forward back over my shoulder.

"Ms. Drake. You need to stop this nonsense at once and

come with us." The burly shifter of the Board—I don't know his name—snaps at me.

"Consider it stopped." Nails digging into the skin of my palms, I bite my tongue. If they think they can blame this on me, they need to think again. "Now call off your goons."

"How dare you ..." the mage stutters as sparks shoot from his fingertips. "None of this would've happened if you didn't spin your ... your..."

"My what?" The circle around me opens, allowing me to step closer to where Fenrir and Astara are standing. "My magic? I'm a mage now, too?" Snickering, I ignore the Fae inching closer to me, mainly because I'm still upset with him for being a jerk to Myst. "The way you people are throwing new things at me, I have a feeling you'll need to build me a shrine pretty soon and worship me like one of the gods." The shifter Board member growls and takes a step towards me, but then he jerks back, almost jumping a foot off the ground when the wolf snarls. The panther's hiss follows directly after.

The Board member glares.

I grin wider.

Movement from the corner of my eye makes my smile falter. Argoz stands between the Board members and Astara, the collar of his shirt gaping open. He must've been pulling on it long enough to make it look almost like he is wearing a V neck. The ghoul's face looks pale and his eyes are too wide for his face, which are darting all over the place. I feel like someone punched me in the stomach.

"Argoz, you went along with this shit?" I can't hide the hurt in my voice to save my life.

Silas smirks, his black pools serving as eyes glittering in triumph.

"Me? No." Argoz takes a step back although I haven't

moved. "Ms. Drake, I tried to stop them. Their arguments, however, have merit ..." He flinches at my glare. "Had merit at the time I should say." The ghoul's shoulders drop and he deflates in front of my eyes. "I don't know what to believe anymore."

"They are turning us against each other." Talking slowly like I'm speaking to a simpleton, I lean slightly forward and pin him under my gaze. "While Roberti is trying to unleash the Titans and humans on us, the hunters are doing their best to kill as many supernaturals as they can." If it's possible, the ghoul pales more. "And you don't know what to believe? How about I don't want any of us to die, least of all me." Argoz tugs on his collar again, and it's obvious he is fighting for breath. Can a ghoul have a panic attack?

If I live a thousand years, I'll never forget the high-pitched squeal Silas makes in that moment.

"Call everyone off, now." Zoltan has his face pressed cheek to cheek with Silas, his fangs a breath away from the Board member's throat. Sharp claws are wrapped around Silas's neck, the tips shredding his skin and rivulets of blood soaking the collar of his shirt. "Or don't," Zoltan whispers just loud enough for us to hear him. "Give me a reason to drain you dry right here, right now."

I have to give it to Silas. The vamp doesn't fold as fast as I think he will. In his shoes, I may be yelling like a fighting match announcer to get everyone's attention so I don't die the moment Zoltan takes me by the neck. I had the male running his hands tenderly over my body and I barely stop myself from emptying my bladder just from the sound of his voice and the hatred gleaming in his gaze right now. But I also know the same hands that worship my body will separate Silas's head from his shoulders if he doesn't speak up soon.

"Zoltan"—Silas swallows embedding the claws deeper into his skin— "I see you are back."

"Not thanks to any of you." Zoltan growls, the words coming from deep in his chest.

Silas locks gazes with the mage and nods slightly, being careful not to nail himself deeper in Zoltan's grip. I stiffen when the mage Board member flings his hand up and sends a blast of magic like a cannonball up in the air. It swirls and pulses for a second before blasting apart with a loud boom that no doubt even the humans hear through the portal. The panther moves fast, preventing me from toppling on the ground when the earth rocks violently.

All fighting stops.

It's the only reason I hear the startled gasp from the shifter Board member. When I turn to look at him, his eyes are comically wide while he stares at the panther with his mouth gaping open. Even Silas looks startled at seeing the large feline. To make things more awkward and take away any points in my favor with the Board, the panther sits primly at my feet, curling his tail around my ankle. His jaw stretches in a yawn wide enough to fit my head inside it before he licks his paw and rubs it over his face.

"It can't be," Argoz gushes reverently, and I look around confused as hell about what's going on.

Everyone is staring at me and the damn panther giving himself a bath at my feet. At least the fighting has stopped, so I'll count the small blessings while I can. When I glance at Zoltan, who is still choking the shit out of Silas, my stomach clenches at the proud smirk on his face. Leo joins me, plopping next to my feet with his upper lip curled, his eyes burning into the Board members.

"Of course, it can." Fenrir sniffs arrogantly, folding his hands at the small of his back like some professor about to give the best lecture of his career. "Anyone want to say anything while we have everyone's attention?" The Fae looks from one grim Beard member to the next. "I didn't think so. Let us take this inside then, shall we?"

Everyone turns as one and moves towards the academy like the high tide of the ocean pushing at the shore. Zoltan leads them dragging Silas by the neck. I stand frozen, my mind empty and unable to think of one reason the air filling my lungs is so potent with excitement and expectancy. I'm not stupid. I know it has something to do with the feline acting dumb at my feet, but for the life of me I can't figure out what. There are tons of shifters here, from wolves to lions, tigers, bears, foxes, and even different types of birds along with the sea creatures. So, what's so special about this one? And why in all the fates do I end up with the animal stuck to my side?

"Let's get inside." Astara links her arm through mine, kicking Leo aside in the process. I notice not even she will walk beside the panther.

"What just happened?" I'm not sure my lips move when I whisper under my breath at Astara, but the feline tilts his head up and I swear he grins at me.

"It's just you being you, Franky." Astara smiles, her eyes crinkling at the corners. "I wish you knew how special you are." Tugging on my arm, she pulls us to follow the others. I force the lump in my throat down.

"Special, my ass," I say so softly there is no way it could've been heard.

When the panther whips his tail across my ass and makes me yelp, I jump and rush forward while Astara chortles. The stupid shifter will leave red welts on my skin for sure.

Chapter Three

"I seriously can't catch a break."

At my muttering, Astara nudges me forward with a sharp jab of her elbow in my ribcage. It irks me to no end that everyone subtly shuffles around and forms a protective barrier between me and the Board members when we enter the open hall. A handful of mages are spread around to keep a crackling barrier that prevents people from attacking each other. Mostly to protect the old farts, as Astara likes to call them, even when they can't free them from Zoltan. Braving the ancient males is not a death wish on my part, but this is getting out of hand. The conversation I had with Fenrir about chess games and chess pieces being moved around the game board is like an insistent mosquito in the back of my mind.

"All hail the queen." Murmuring under my breath, I snicker like an idiot, wiping my sweaty palms on the fabric of my borrowed pants.

"What?" The deep frown pulling Astara's thin eyebrows

low over her eyes may be comical if every eye in the large space isn't trained on me.

"Never mind." A few people do a double take when I force my lips to stretch into a smile.

"Don't," Astara mumbles, huffing when I quirk an eyebrow at her. "Just … don't smile, okay? You look constipated. Leave the resting bitch face in place. It's way more natural."

"Gee, thanks. Picking up tricks from Myst, or did you come up with that insult all on your own?" Dodging people, I weave through the crowd so I can reach Fenrir and Leo, my friend hot on my heels the whole way. "I really feel the love. Don't sugarcoat things on my account."

"Trust me on this, Franky. I know these things, so you just continue to glare at them. It'll do the trick." She grins like a fool when I jerk my head back to stare at her. "Exactly like that."

Shaking my head at her antics instead of watching where I'm going, the tip of my shoe bumps into someone's foot. Twisting my ankle so I don't step on their toes, I trip over my own feet, my stomach dropping to my feet when I pitch forward for the second time tonight. A hand wraps around the back of my shirt to stop my fall, the sound of fabric ripping shooting through the room like a gun going off.

"Easy, Hellion." Fenrir materializes next to me and yanks me up, his fingers digging into my upper arms. "You good?" Flinching back when the panther growls deep in his throat, the Fae eyes the cat warily.

"Yup." My voice is shaky from the heartbeat strangling my throat. "I tripped," I add stupidly like there is a single person in this room that has missed my clumsy maneuver.

A choking sound makes me peer behind me, my face

catching fire when I see Astara fighting a laugh. Swallowing thickly in hopes to push the drumming of my heart where it belongs, I fidget with my shirt and try to straighten it, which is an impossible task since the seams of the collar are ripped thanks to Astara grabbing me from behind. After a moment I give up, grimacing when the front drapes over my boobs. *At least I'm not naked,* I tell myself and lift my chin up, ignoring the continuing snorts coming from my friend. Fenrir's lips twitch but he schools his features fast when I scowl at him.

"If you are done with the show, Ms. Drake, we are waiting." Silas sneers as he stands next to the far wall of the hall.

"No monkeys, no circus." Chirping cheerfully just to piss him off, I stride with determined steps right at him.

It works.

As soon as those standing between us part, all three Board members' faces twist with different levels of disdain. The old Francesca would've tucked tail and bolted out of here as fast as her feet would carry her. If for nothing else, I do miss my old self for her ignorance in so many things. But that person is long gone. Soren made sure she retreated so far inside me I can barely feel the echoes of who I used to be.

My chin tilts up a notch higher.

Taking a lesson from Fenrir's book, I look down my nose at the three assholes. With their misguided ideals, they're willing to let all of us kill each other as long as it leaves them at the top of the food chain. If I didn't know better, I may think they are in cahoots with Roberti. I'm still not one-hundred percent sure they're not. A knot forms in the pit of my stomach, twisting and shredding my insides.

I hope I'm wrong. Please, fates, make sure I'm wrong.

"Now what?" Aiming my question at Silas, I breathe

easier when Zoltan glides gracefully from behind the vampire to stand next to me. Little zaps of electric currents slither under my skin where the back of his hand brushes mine.

"I would choose my next words wisely." Zoltan's voice is even, his words softly spoken, but their impact is as if he has roared them in their faces.

"You are forgetting your place, Zoltan." Anger tightens the edges of the mage's mouth.

"Like a fledgling losing his path over a ..." Silas chokes, his nails scratching and clawing at his throat. The shifter and the mage pale, the color draining from their faces, while the vampire Board member purples like an eggplant.

With a sigh like he's dealing with misbehaving children, Zoltan folds his arms across his chest. All my girly bits tingle from the way he is throwing off alpha vibes. Squirming, I press my thighs together and pray to whoever listens that no one can scent my arousal. *Perfect timing, Franky ...you idiot,* I chide myself. Astara's sharp nail stabbing me between the ribs gets my brain back online.

"Let him speak, Zoltan." No matter how much I hate these three, the last thing we need is Zoltan killing Silas for being a dumb jerk. "It's not like he'll say anything I haven't heard before."

It takes a long moment, and the silence is so oppressive my shoulders ache from the density of it before Silas gasps, gulping air while trying not to cough out a lung. A look passes between the shifter and the mage warning me that the game has changed. Zoltan stiffens next to me, his shoulders pulling back just a bit, and that tells me he catches it, too. The fact that I notice these tiny details about him and know what they mean is something I'll think on later, like when I'm alone and can hit my head off a wall for being stupid enough to allow him to get under my skin.

"You were looking for me like I'm some wanted criminal, or a fugitive." Turning from one to the other, I make sure the Board member's attention shifts to me. "Instead of waiting for me to come back so we can discuss whatever has you riled up, you thought it would be better to get people to start attacking each other. The same people you harbor here to protect, the ones who protect you in return. Well, here I am." A tired sigh escapes me and I glare at all three of them. "Let's hear my crimes." Silas sucks in a breath and opens his mouth, but I cut him off before he begins. "And don't start with being a half blood because that's old news."

Astara chuckles.

"Don't you see them thumping their fists over their hearts? Swearing loyalty to you like some savior that will lead them to glory? Rules have been put in place and obeyed for centuries for a reason, Ms. Drake." It's the shifter that speaks, his voice rumbling deep in his chest like rolling rocks. I need to ask what their names are eventually or I'll start calling them jerk one and jerk two. "They are there not just to protect us, but to protect the humans as well. Yet here you are, turning everything on its head that we have fought so hard to build with our blood, sweat, and tears. Destroying everything we stand for. Your misguided heroics by rushing into unknown battles placed the academy in a very difficult place. You divided us, and the Board will not stand for it."

"Last time I checked it was you who bound me to this damn place without asking permission. Meanwhile, while I was out there trying to bring one of your strongest back because he was taken from right under your noses, you decided I was breaking your stupid rules?" The shifter hunches forward, his narrow gaze turning his eyes into slits. "I did nothing but my best to protect Sienna, and by default everyone on this side of the portal. Where were you while the rest of us were fighting for our lives?"

"Do not make this some self-sacrificing quest to save us all, Ms. Drake." The mage slashes his hand through the air with finality. "Whatever it is between you and Roberti does not matter. You dragged the academy in the middle of it. Some of us can see right through your innocent act."

"Do you listen to the crap that comes out of your mouth?" My body trembles from the anger churning inside me. The skin on my arm and the right side of my face stings from the power blasting at me from Zoltan and Fenrir, their rage as strong as my own. "My act? Innocents were dying in Sienna while you were sitting cozy on your chairs pretending to see nothing. If you are accusing me of doing everything I can to put an end to it, then I'm guilty as charged. But don't you dare pin what has been happening under your watch while you were looking the other way on me. Aren't you the almighty Daywalkers? Aren't you supposed to be protecting us all? Where were you when Sienna needed you?" I scream the last words in their faces, my throat raw from the injustice of their accusations.

"No!" I whirl on Zoltan when he takes a step forward, his fangs bared at the Board. "I don't need you to fight my battles. Let them sling their facts at me. Let them tell me what I have done wrong without some made up bullshit."

"You divided the academy," Silas snarls, spittle flying from his mouth. "They will follow you to their doom and give the hunters the chance to finally put an end to us all. Is that what you want?"

"Listen asshole."—The colors shift in front of my eyes, rage bringing my magic to the surface no matter how hard I try to push it back. All three old males take a step back before catching themselves. "I had a very long week. I haven't slept without seeing the blade under Zoltan's throat or Roberti's gloating face when he threatened to expose us all. I haven't eaten, and I was fighting for my life as well as Zoltan's until a few hours ago almost destroying those hunters you claim I'm somehow helping to destroy you. So, unless you can tell me what you did to help, or exactly what you want from me, I'm done fucking talking."

The air is whistling through my nostrils as I pant clenching my fists so hard, I can feel blood trickling in rivulets from my palms. We stare at each other, them watching me like some ticking bomb that's about to go off, and me debating the pros and cons of snapping their necks. It won't kill them but it'll give me some satisfaction at least. The panther bristles beside me, shrieking a vicious cry, and my heart jerks in my chest before hammering my ribs.

"This got a bit out of control." The mage changes gears like I change socks and it leaves me gaping at him. I blink dumbly at his serene face.

"You think?" Astara chirps dryly from behind me, and she gets three matching glares in response.

"What we are saying is you cannot divide us if we are to protect Sienna, Ms. Drake." The shifter startles at Zoltan's growl. With all the sounds around me, it's like animal kingdom in here. "Zoltan, hear me out. We have a solution to all this." The burly male opens his arms palms up, placating us as if we are making the problems.

"Let me guess." Breathing through my nose so I can calm down, I crack my neck but it doesn't help to relieve the pressure building behind my eyeballs. "It involves me bleeding to death or being chained up somewhere. Am I getting close?"

"Preposterous." The mage even looks taken aback, and I almost laugh in his face.

Almost.

"No one can undo what Soren did by binding you to him, and by default to the academy." I have to give it to Silas, he tries really hard not to show how much it pains him to say this. The grimace on his face is a dead giveaway on how he feels, however. "So we came up with a solution where we can all work together for the same goal." I open my mouth but his scowl makes the words die on my tongue. "It doesn't involve you bleeding to death"—I swear he licks his lips, the creep— "or being chained anywhere. It's much simpler than that."

"And less messy," the mage pipes in with a leer.

"No." Zoltan and Fenrir bellow at once, and I jump out of my skin at the sudden shout.

"It'll solve everything, and we can focus on the hunters. She will have our full support." Silas is smiling like he just won the lotto and was proclaimed the king of the world.

My stomach drops to my feet, bile burning the back of my throat.

"No," Zoltan hisses, taking a menacing step towards the Board members.

"Let her decide, Zoltan. Let everyone that followed her to the human realm and is willing to fight for her hear what she will choose. Let them see who they pledge loyalty to." Silas turns to me smugly, and I know before he even speaks that no matter what I answer I'll just be stepping deeper into my freshly-dug grave. "All this can be avoided if you take the oath and get initiated in the Daywalker's guild, Ms. Drake."

Something deep inside me shrinks back at his words.

"Show that you will pledge your life to protect them like

26

they are placing theirs in your hands." The asshole looks eager as he leans forward. "Everything you have said is just words. But taking the oath will prove those words aren't empty promises."

The pressure behind my eyes intensifies. Everyone around me is shouting, trying to be heard over all the voices in the room. My gaze locks on Silas's, his soulless eyes boring into mine like he wants to see my soul. The corners of his thin lips lift in a smug smile, telling me he thinks he won by giving me this ultimatum. He expects me to decline.

My gaze roams the room meeting worried glances all around, but the panther's eyes make me freeze. The feline is watching me with a calm and level gaze, and the knot in my stomach loosens. I'm not sure why, but I know deep inside that no matter what they want me to do, everything will be okay at the end. I might not come out the same on the other side but if that will get the Board off my back so I can get to Roberti, it'll be worth it. If it'll protect my friends and prevent more deaths, no matter what they want from me will be worth it. I know I should ask what giving an oath entails, but at this point there's no reason. I can't see a way around it without causing more harm than necessary.

"I'll do it."

You can hear a pin drop.

It's almost like the academy itself is holding its breath at my murmured words. When the yelling resumes with more intensity, Astara joins Zoltan and Fenrir and slings threats at the three old jerks. A rock drops in my gut. What the hell did I just agree to?

Chapter Four

A soft breeze follows the cracking of the wood when the door to my room opens. Every nerve ending in my body tunes in to Zoltan even before he steps foot inside, the metal of the door handle groaning under his tight grip. As if I don't know he is pissed at me for playing along with the stupid games the Board is shoving down my throat. I rushed out of the grand hall while they were still arguing, unwilling to watch them rip each other's throat's out. My adrenaline rush limit has been reached, that's for sure. It was either stay there and faint like some weakling, or leave and crawl into my room like a wounded puppy.

I chose the latter.

Fingers absently tracing patterns over the panther's fur, I stare at the ceiling. My entire body protests when I fling myself on the bed, and now the purr coming from the shifter, who has crawled on my side, is soothing like the constant rumble of an idling engine. I can feel it in the center of my chest and it keeps me calm for whatever reason.

But all my Zen disappears when Zoltan snarls, and every bit of calm I feel dissipates as Fenrir shoulders his way inside. Astara and Leo are right behind him.

"The meeting room is down the hall to your left, in case you all got lost on your way there," I tell the ceiling, sounding tired even to my own ears.

"You know he is not an animal." Zoltan glares at the giant cat stretched out next to me.

"If you can get him out of here, be my guest." The purr kicks up a notch, vibrating my insides. "I didn't have the will or the strength today to wrestle with him at the door."

With a shriek, I flail when Zoltan plucks me off the bed before situating himself over it, his back pressed on the headboard and plopping me in his lap. The panther grumbles but his head stays down, his paws tucked under his chin. Only his ear flicks left and right, his intent gaze not straying from me.

"At least I don't get the urge to put the shifter on a leash so he behaves." I huff squirming in a futile attempt to free myself of the frustrating Daywalker.

"You want to put a leash on me?" Zoltan's hot breath tickles my skin, his low words meant just for me melting my insides. Emotions clog my throat and prevent me from breathing. Wetting my parched mouth with my tongue, I avoid looking at the others in fear of what I'll see.

"You are not going through with the initiation," Fenrir says, his words cutting through my thoughts like a blade. Astara is already shaking her head, yet none of it helps me forget the fact that Zoltan's is wrapped around me like a boa.

"I need to leave the academy." I change the subject before my hormones make me do something stupid, like rub all over Zoltan as if I'm a bitch in heat for example.

All the oxygen in the room is sucked out.

"Hear me out." I silence whatever protests coming my way with a hand when I hear the collective intake of air. "I don't mean leave as in walk out and never return. I need to go to Sienna." Twisting around and doing my best to ignore the rock-hard erection poking my hip, I lock eyes with Zoltan.

"You know what happened when you tried to leave." His blue gaze is searching but I can see his unwillingness to let me go, too.

"How can I ever forget." If my words were any dryer ash would spew from my lips.

I shiver in Zoltan's arms when the sound of whistling wind through the forest while I run faster than I've ever done before deafens me. The memory of that night claws its way to the surface, the humidity of the air choking me even now as moisture fills my lungs. The stench of rotting roots and moist soil fills my nostrils and I gasp for air to remind myself I'm not sprawled face down on the forest floor slowly dying while staring at the iron gates so close yet too far to reach.

"Francesca." Zoltan's arms tighten around me. "Look at me." When I don't comply fast enough for his tastes, he shakes me so hard it rattles my bones, but it snaps me out of the panic. "Ms. Drake, breathe!"

"Seriously, you need to stop"—Gulping air, I push on his chest to get up but my attempts don't even register with him— "calling me ... Ms. Drake. Or get the hell out of my bed, and room while you're at it."

"If you push your luck you can announce your celibacy starting now." Fenrir guffaws, which in turn makes Leo belt out a laugh that startles the panther.

"I need to go to Sienna," I repeat, not letting them side-track me.

"What is this desire to go to Sienna all of a sudden, Hellion?" Fenrir crosses one ankle over the other and leans back on the wall next to my door while I listen to Zoltan's teeth grinding from behind me. "We have enough problems to deal with here."

"I need to see Daren." Ignoring the vamp turning into granite under me, I keep my gaze level with the Fae. "I must talk to him ... alone."

After I sneaked out from the hall, I couldn't shake the idea that I should speak to Daren. Everyone here has shared details of what is going on and clued me in on many things, but they all have given an oath preventing them from sharing too much. I still feel like I'm on a need to know basis, and with the Board cornering me into this initiation, I have to be prepared for whatever they throw at me. I trust Zoltan, Astara, and Fenrir, as well as Leo, but I don't trust them not to be biased. They are Daywalkers after all. Fighting Roberti, Cassius, and Alex is one thing, but the academy as a whole is a totally different matter. Will they be willing to stand against what they are if it comes down to it? Will they pick my side, the side of a half blood—dragon blood or not—when every-thing they've known for centuries is this? My mage friend, however, has no qualms about exposing all their dirty secrets, especially if he knows my life might depend on it. Before I get myself in a deeper hole, I have to hear what he says.

"You can't leave." Zoltan sounds too casual with his words, but I can feel him coiled up like a snake ready to bite. "We can get the mage here if you wish to speak with him."

"Right, because he will be thrilled to come to the one

place he hates more than anything in the worlds." Glancing at Astara, I judge her reaction to see if I'll get any help from her in this. "They took the love of his life from him, and you honestly think anything can convince him to cross those gates?"

"If he is your friend, he will do it for you." A strange look crosses Fenrir's face, leaving me wondering if he is implying that he is a better friend than Daren. Who knows, though? Maybe it just bothers him that he isn't.

"Even the trees have ears here, so I need to speak with him on his terms. Otherwise, he won't tell me anything. Bringing him here is not an option. I need to go to him." My mind is already spinning with a plan to get my ass to Daren's pub. If it comes to it, I'll wake Soren up because the ancient Fae will have a way. I know that much.

"You don't trust us." Lifting me off him, Zoltan stands up and sets me on the bed, not meeting my eyes. "Not fully."

"I don't think that's what—" Astara frowns at her brother's back when he yanks the door open.

"I know what she's saying," he cuts her off. "I just thought …" My insides twist into a knot when his shoulders snap back. The Zoltan I met the first day I arrived at the academy makes an appearance. The air around him shifts, closing him off from me. "You cannot leave the grounds, Ms. Drake. For your sake, of course, but also for everyone else's you need to stay away from those gates."

My chest hollows, numbness spreading through me like a wave. He doesn't say Ms. Drake in a teasing matter like he normally does just to irk me. This is more like shutting a door in my face, making it loud and clear what will happen if I disobey his orders. Anger festers in my stomach, more at myself than at Zoltan. What did I think? That just because I allowed him inside my body, he would follow my wishes and think of me before anything else? Tears prick my eyes, the room and everyone in it blurring for a second. I blink them away and clench my jaw. It's good to put this distance between us from the start. My stupid heart might confuse lust for love and that will be the end of me. Ancient oaths, death threats, and old males on a power trip I can live with.

But loving Zoltan will kill me without a doubt.

"As much as I hate him right now for being a typical stubborn male, I have to agree with my brother, Franky." Astara implores me with her eyes as she wrings her fingers. "After what we did to Roberti, even if you could go down to Sienna, I'd rather you didn't. He has spies everywhere, not just at the academy. If he gets you alone he will jump at the chance."

The headache I've been fighting intensifies. It's not that I want to put myself in a peculiar position by seeking to see Daren. I need to speak with him without worrying if we will be overheard. Plus, I don't have it in me to ask him to step foot here after everything he's told me about the woman he loved and how much he still suffers from losing her. Do I have the right to disturb his life? Remembering the look on Silas's face like a vulture about to get a feast, I have to admit the three jerks got one thing right …

I am selfish.

Maybe even Zoltan is right in thinking I'm cunning. At the end of the day, I don't want to die, and I'm willing to go to great lengths to prevent it from happening. I can feel the weight of Fenrir's gaze drilling a whole on the side of my face, but I don't look at him. Instead, my attention goes to Leo. The alpha is usually very chatty, making fun of everyone just to lighten things. Yet, he has barely said a word this whole time.

"What's up, mutt? No smartass remarks for me?" A lump forms in my throat when he blinks solemnly at me, sadness blanketing his features. "You not gonna try to stop me?"

"No." His voice is thick, so he clears his throat a couple of times. "Before you even neared our gates, they've been surrounding you from all sides, guiding you into a corner where they know you can't escape." My heart skips a beat when he voices all my fears, not looking away from me. "Not just Roberti, but the Board, too, and even Soren himself. You want to know why it bothers the Board that everyone rushed to have your back and you instigated this new order, Drake?"

Internally I'm screaming for him to shut his mouth and not say another word, but on the outside, I stare at him numbly and shake my head jerkily at his question. Astara stares at her feet with a frown tugging her eyebrows down, while if Fenrir wasn't breathing, I may think he's turned into a mannequin.

"Because while cornered and thinking you are fighting just for yourself, you never leave anyone behind. They don't understand the concept and see it as a manipulation or a trick. Their minds don't work the same way yours does. So, I'm not going to stop you. What I'll do is go talk to your friend down in Sienna and see if he has a solution to our little problem." Lacing his fingers, he stretches his arms over his head. "If nothing else, at least he will know you are looking for a way to get in touch with him. A real friend, one you trust, won't even think of the reasons he hates this place if you are in danger."

"Tell him Franky said the drinks are on me next time I come to the pub. He will know you are telling him the truth," I call after Leo as he walks out of my room.

"You have to appreciate it when the mention of alcohol tells someone the message is from you." Astara snorts after Fenrir follows Leo and closes the door behind them.

"Daren warned me a long time ago about Roberti. I was pissed off at him for months before deciding he is just too bitter and it's not worth ignoring him for it."

"What did he warn you about?"

"He said a moron can see Roberti is manipulating you and has an agenda when it comes to you. You are just too desperate to belong that you are blind to it. But, it's all good. When you finally see it, the drinks are on you the moment you step foot in my pub." A smile tilts my lips and Astara matches it. "Daren will forget anything, but he will never forget a promised drink. I just hope he knows a way we can talk."

"The initiation requires a sacrifice, Franky." Astara fists her hands. "We will find a way out of it."

It's like she punched me in the center of my chest. The sharp pain spreads but I manage to give her a smile, albeit a fake one. Daren better find a way to see me or I'm royally screwed this time.

Chapter Five

Swallowing thickly, I raise my fist for the fifth time, hesitating again because I'm unable to summon the strength to knock on Zoltan's door. I know he is inside; I can feel him through his blood still coursing inside me, just as he is aware that I'm standing here like a lump and have been for the last fifteen minutes. It doesn't help me suck it up and storm inside to demand he talk to me. He has no right to be upset that I want to speak to my friend alone. *Keep telling yourself that if it makes you feel better.* Even my inner voice is snide, and it makes me grind my teeth.

My clenched fist falls limply to my side and I rub my aching shoulder which has cramped because I'm a coward. Who would've thought, huh? All my bravado went down the drain after I stupidly let myself get too close to the Daywalker. When my skin prickles, pebbling all over my arms and legs, the breath gets stuck in my throat. I can feel him standing just on the other side, the thick wood not enough of a barrier between us. Heart rattling my bones like a war drum, I spin on my heel, ready to bolt out of the eerily silent hallway. Then the door opens, and I'm frozen under Zoltan's solemn gaze.

"Ummm ..." My eyes dart around, panic choking the shit out of me, so I round on the panther who is looking way too smug as he watches me struggle. "There you are." Giggling nervously, I make a big show of flicking my hand at Zoltan's face while his eyes are narrowing by the second. "I thought I lost the damn cat. I didn't want him walking around on his own with the Board ..."

A shrill sound comes out of me when Zoltan strikes like a snake and lifts me off the ground. He yanks me inside his room, slamming the door in the panther's face with a resounding boom. The feline and I growl incredulously at the same time, but he only leans back on the door, his intent gaze never leaving my face. Short of breath, my chest rises and falls in shallow bursts of air, and I smooth nonexistent hairs out of my face with shaking hands.

"Stop manhandling me you ... you ... Neanderthal." The corners of his full lips twitch when I take a step away from him. "In this day and age, we use words to communicate."

"That only works, Francesca, if the female is not hell bent on going against what's good for her." The arrogant jerk folds his arms across his massive chest, his biceps pulling on the fabric of his shirt. I raise my hand to check for a drool before I catch what I'm doing and glare at him.

The smirk grows on his stupidly handsome face.

"Did you put the book behind wards?" Picking the safest option for a conversation, I decide to ignore his smoldering gaze and move around his room.

"No, I'll keep it close until we are sure no one can get their hands on it."

"In other words, you'll keep it until Roberti is dealt

with." Finding a neatly-stacked pile of books, I nudge the middle spine with a finger and pointedly stare at Zoltan over my shoulder. It'll drive Mr. OCD insane to mess up his neat things.

A muscle jumps in his jaw.

Gloating, I'm thrilled to ruffle his feathers.

"You were not standing in the hallway to ask about the book." Nostrils flaring, I can see how much it costs him not to move and put the books back the way they were.

Shrugging a shoulder, I poke at the pile some more before moving further inside the room. "Leo and Fenrir are in Sienna, and Astara left to get a feel of the situation among our ranks. Her words not mine. We didn't get a chance to talk about what our next move is, so I figured now is as good of a time as any to hush out what the plan is. After the display the Board gave us, I don't think we have much time to do anything before they stick their noses in our business."

Pretending I don't hear the low growl coming from deep in his chest, I touch everything I can get my hands on, shifting things slightly just so they are moved from their original place. Consciously, I know I'm poking at a sleeping lion, but I can't help myself. Feeing unsettled because he was hurt earlier by my words makes me act irrational. And here I am thinking I grew out of my self-destructive ways. I guess some things we never learn.

"You are worried about their loyalty." It's not a question, so I just offer a twitchy shrug eyeing him warily to judge his reaction.

Will he hate me for stirring the pot, turning his entire existence upside down? I don't know how old he is but I don't need a number to know that the Daywalker Academy is his life mission, something that he lives and breathes. And here I am, a half blood popping out of nowhere wreaking chaos while pointing an accusing finger at his friends, at his family. Zoltan's expression gives nothing away to let me know how he feels about it.

I force down the lump the size of a fist in my throat.

Pushing off the door, he sighs and stabs his hands in the pockets of his pants. "You know what bothers me more than doubting everything I've ever known?" I stiffen when he moves but he just strides to his large bed and perches on the edge of it, his intent focus like a physical weight on my shoulders. "After everything that's happened, you still don't trust me … not fully."

"Just because we had sex doesn't mean anything has changed." A humorless smile tilts his lips at my words. My insides are knotted so tight, I'm worried I'll empty my stomach where I stand.

"Is that what we did? We had sex?" By the sound of it, I came here to clear the air for hurting him earlier, but I did the opposite of that.

Scrubbing a hand roughly over my face, I turn away so he doesn't see how his words affect me. "What I'm trying to say is, I don't expect you to back me up on all my assumptions. Because let's face it, until I have solid evidence any of them are working with Roberti, all I'm doing is conjuring."

"I have sex when I need to scratch an itch." Like a dog with a bone, he ignores everything I just said.

"Which you've done plenty." Cringing internally, I keep digging a deeper hole because I have no control of my mouth. "You must've had an allergy or something …" Squeezing my eyes shut, I bite my tongue to shut myself up. *Way to go dumbass, you couldn't be more obvious that you care.*

My breath gets stuck when Zoltan wraps my braid around his fist and jerks me around to face him. I didn't even hear him move. I'm left speechless when my eyes snap open from the pulsing glow of his own. The blue in his irises shifts from dark indigo to silver and back, mesmerizing me. Like two magnets, our bodies pull us together out of our control, the press of his hard chest making me melt against him. My knees wobble and I'm grateful for his hold on my hair or I would be a puddle at his feet.

"In the many years I have walked this world I have, yes." His gaze searches mine, although I'm unfocused, dazed by the potent power coming off of him in sharp bursts. "But nothing can compare to being with you, Francesca Drake. I don't think it's a good thing for you to know what you do to me." The rumble in his chest sounds so primal the short hairs on the back of my neck lift at attention. "I've never allowed anyone to have that much power."

"You don't let anyone have power over you, Daywalker." What I was hoping to sound like a snappy retort turned into a moan. Kill me now.

"I don't." He nips my lower lip and liquid heat pools at my core. "And then there is you. You have no idea how special you are." His breath puffs over my lips.

"I wish people would stop saying that," I mumble, still locked in his piercing gaze. "I'm no one."

"The fact that you believe that makes you very danger-ous." His full mouth curls into a hungry smile, the tip of a fang poking under his upper lip sending my heart somer-saulting. "I like it, you just need to learn one thing."

The anger I usually feel at his arrogance mixes with my arousal and muddles my brain. My palm is itching to slap that smile off his face but the sharp curve of his cheekbones and his thick lashes, which are throwing shadows over them like crescent moons, leave me blinking slowly, basking in the sound of his thundering heart. It matches my own. My lips part the tongue wetting them, wishing for him to close the barely-there distance and kiss me.

With a snarl, Zoltan flips me around, my pants along with his own disappearing with a sharp tug of his wrist. All my protests die on my tongue when he enters me in one hard thrust, pinning me on the end of the bed. I can feel him everywhere. His shaft is stretching me to bursting, but his large body curled around mine sucks all the oxygen from my lungs. His scent fills my nostrils and silences all thought. Fear sparks inside me that I will lose myself, the feeling of him so potent that it's drowning me in who and what Zoltan is. Stiffening, I lock my knees to shove him off me, but he moves.

There is no sign of the gentle lover from the shower. With my hair still wrapped around his fist and his other hand clamped on my hip, Zoltan starts pounding me into the mattress. My lips part in a silent scream, his grunts and snarls stroking the fire burning in my belly into an inferno. Each time his powerful thighs slap the back of my own it's like he is branding himself on my skin. The rough skin of his palm scrapes over my skin, his fingers digging into my hip as if I'm trying to escape. There is no running away from this even if I try.

Zoltan is proving a point.

I like to tell myself I regret my snarky remark about his prowls, but with each glide of his cock inside me my low moans and screams join his groans to create a song as old as time itself. The part of me that wants to keep the Daywalker even when she knows she never could luxuriate in his strength and dominance, preening because she can make him lose control. He told me I have power over him, but he is showing me now that he has the same influence over me. The first time we were skin to skin, he enjoyed my body as much as I enjoyed his. That was two people coming together, intimately joining their bodies. This is not the same.

This is a claiming.

Zoltan yanks my head back, crushing his mouth over mine. His tongue pushes through my lips, licking and sucking, scraping the smooth tissue with the tips of his fangs. Twisting the sheets in my hands I push back in sync with his trusts, wanting him harder and deeper inside me until I don't know where he ends and I begin. He gives me what I need and more, stealing my heart one mingled breath at a time.

Pressure builds in my lower belly, sparking the power in my chest to pulse with the beat of each pump from Zoltan's hips. He moves faster, his sack slapping a staccato over my ass, and I relish in it. The low growl coming from his chest like an idling engine gets louder, spurring my moans. He releases my mouth, tilting my head to the side and sinking his fangs as long as my pinky in my neck.

Stars burst behind my closed eyelids, my channel clamping tightly on his cock and milking him. He gets thicker and harder inside me, hot steel pounding the mouth of my womb without missing a beat. My blood rushes down his throat and his lips press firmer on my skin with each suction he makes. It's like he is draining all my fight along with my soul, drinking it in so I can never get away from him. His rhythm falters, his movements turning erratic and jerky before he lurches his head back, his deafening roar rattling the windows. Hot spurts bathe my insides, forcing another orgasm stronger than the previous one. Darkness is trying to pull me under, creeping inside my head because the pleasure is too much to bear.

Zoltan crushes me to his chest, his arms wrapping around me like metal bands the only thing keeping me from passing out. "Do what you want to do, Francesca." His deep voice is raw, pebbling my skin. "But don't you ever forget that you are mine."

"You wish." I'm not sure I actually manage to say it out loud before I pass out.

Chapter Six

All my fantasies about sneaking out of Zoltan's bed and bolting out of the room vanish the second I twitch a muscle. The thick arm that is thrown over my waist like a dead-weight tightens as soon as my breathing changes. I have a moment to freak the hell out about having the Daywalker spooning me before I want to punch him in the throat.

He chuckles.

"There is not one thing I find funny right now." Wiggling proves to be a bad idea when I feel him harden, his erection poking my lower back.

I freeze.

"What's the matter, Drake," Zoltan rasps, his voice brimming with amusement and thick from sleep. "Not enjoying the fact that you're caught?"

"Get over yourself, I wasn't running so you could catch me." Nope, not even flailing helps. He just yanks me tighter to his chest. Huffing, I give up on my attempt to get away from him. "What are we doing Zoltan? Our world is burning and here we are playing house."

"Is that what we are doing?" He grunts when I elbow him.

"Don't be an ass, you know what I mean." Gnawing on the inside of my mouth, I can't get rid of the guilt eating a hole in my stomach. People are getting hurt while I'm enjoying myself snuggling with Zoltan in our fake bubble of calm.

"There will always be someone disturbing our lives, Francesca." His voice is soft, vibrating from his chest into my back. "If we allow them to steal our little moments of peace, they've already won."

"You sound like Soren." Grumbling petulantly, I'd be lying if I said he didn't have a point. Not that I'll tell him that. He is arrogant enough to last a few lifetimes. "You two should compare notes."

"What notes would those be?" Nuzzling my hair, which is spread out like a cloud around my head, somehow unbound from the braid, he breathes me in. "Teaming Francesca Drake for beginners?"

"Ha, ha!" I say dryly, pressing deeper in the pillow, but he doesn't allow me to pull away from him. "Very funny. You should be a comedian. You'll make it big in the human world in no time."

"I'll keep it in mind if this Daywalker business doesn't pan out." I look over my shoulder when he deadpans, thoughtful and even. "I'll hire you as an agent. I'll pay good money to see anyone try to negotiate with you."

"Did you just make a joke?" He blinks his eyes open lazily, just a sliver of blue peeking through his long lashes. "The end of the worlds is coming. The great Zoltan, aka one-word wonder, has a sense of humor."

"I'm finding I've had a lot of firsts since you fell at my

feet." A slow smile tilts his lips, erupting butterflies in my belly.

"I tripped asshole, don't flatter yourself. You just happened to be there when I lost my balance." I can feel the heat creeping over my face, so I duck my head to hide from his knowing gaze.

"Mhm," he rumbles, spreading goosebumps over my skin like a blanket. "I can hear you even now whispering 'surprise.'" My body rocks on the mattress from his chuckle. "What a surprise you turned out to be indeed."

"Right." Face on fire, I'm left lost for a response as I try to ignore my insides, which are melting at his words. I'll have no one else to blame but myself when he rips my heart apart, but I'll tuck that away for now and worry about it later.

"I'm thinking of keeping the book within reach at all times until we put an end to Roberti's insanity. The more I think about it, the bigger the nagging feeling grows inside me that is telling me someone else is pulling his strings."

Zoltan sounds wide awake now and it takes me a little time to get my mind back on track. His naked body plastered to mine from neck to toes doesn't help me at all, especially when he places my soles on top of his feet like it's the most natural thing in the world.

"Andrius doesn't need anyone else feeding his ego, Zoltan. Trust me, I should know." Pushing down the giddy feeling that this is what a real relationship feels like, sharing your inner thoughts while cuddling naked under the sheets, I force myself to concentrate on what he is saying. "If there was any chance that something would give him more power and control over us, he would take it, even at the cost of his soul. It's who he is. Roberti loves knowing he is above everyone."

"He *was* above everyone." I'm already shaking my head before he has finished his sentence.

"Above even you?" His grunt is answer enough. "I didn't think so. It never sat well with him that the academy was holding their power over his head. When I think back now, many things make sense."

"Like?" He pulls away, rolling me on my back. Lifting on one elbow, he glances down at me. "Do you remember seeing him dealing with someone we can look into?"

"You are very chatty all of a sudden. I never pegged you as a morning person." Although I'm grumbling, I can't help but offer a small smile in answer of his open grin.

It's not his well-known smirk or practiced tilt of his lips. What I see in front of me is unguarded and open. It takes my breath away. It smooths the tight, stern lines on his face while making him look boyish and unjaded. My chest tightens. Is this how he would always have been if we lived in different times and a different place? The sparkle in his blue eyes turns searching, so I shake away the direction my thoughts take. Wishful thinking never helps anyone.

"I'm always chatty with the right motivation." He winks, giving me tachycardia.

"All I have to do is get naked, huh? Good to know."

"We are getting somewhere already." Lowering his head slowly and giving me time to move away if I want to, he presses a soft kiss on my lips. "I will never let anything happen to you if I can help it."

"For the millionth time, I don't need you to protect me." I glare at him.

"What do you need, Francesca?" His eyes flick between mine and I can tell he really wants the answer to that question. I wish I knew what I want, although I doubt I will tell him even if I do.

"To stop Roberti." When his guarded gaze turns on me and he is closed off once more, I know that's the wrong answer. It physically hurts me to witness it but it's for the best.

At least that's what I keep telling myself.

One day I might even believe it.

"We will stop him." My heart jerks at the menace in his voice. "He will pay for everything he's done."

Shadows slither behind his eyes, reminding me that until a day ago he was held prisoner, turned feral, and locked in a cage. Something like that can even change a person as strong as Zoltan. As much as I hate Andrius for what he's done and is still doing, I do feel sorry for him because when the Daywalker gets his hands on him, it won't be pretty. My old boss will regret the day he crossed the academy gates.

"We should go and see if Leo and Fenrir are back." Expecting a smartass remark, I'm surprised when Zoltan gives me a sharp nod, rolling off the bed and lifting on his feet.

My mouth goes dry when he stretches his gloriously naked body, the silver light of the moon casting a mesmerizing glow over it through the windows. Shadows form dips and bumps, luring my eyes to different parts of him while he stands still, his gaze locked on my face. I'm not fast enough to school my features and hide the desire burning inside me. Throwing caution to the wind, I let him see how his impossibly-perfect body affects me. His erection thickens in reaction to my perusal.

"Keep looking at me like that and we will never leave this room." His soft voice holds the promise of sweaty skin and unbearable pleasure. I have to swallow the thickness clogging my throat.

"Let's put an end to Roberti and get the Board off my

back first." Gulping when his body coils as if he's preparing to pounce on me, I take a deep breath and release it slowly, my feet wrapping the sheet around my body to hide my nakedness from him. "We can get back to staying in this room for a while after that." My smile wobbles slightly but thankfully he doesn't comment on it.

"I'll remind you of this."

"I don't doubt you will."

We are quiet, each lost in our own thoughts while we shower and dress, the tension saturating the room like a cloud. I end up wearing another pair of Zoltan's pants since mine ended up ripped on the floor. There is something very intimate in wearing clothing from a male after a night of passion. More so than sharing yourself with him. I'm not sure I understand it myself but it gives me tingles in the center of my chest, and the entity sharing my body purrs like a contented cat at the thought. Fenrir says me and the dragon blood are one and the same, but I still don't agree. We have too different of a thought process for that to be true, plus our views on the world don't mesh well, either. It may be the difference between human and animalistic reasoning but I push it away for now. She likes that Zoltan takes what he wants without a care of how that may bite me in the ass in the end. I, on the other hand, would like not to be heartbroken if I can help it. *Right, because you are doing a bang-up job so far.* I flick a quick glance at the rumpled bed before squeezing my eyes shut, the memories of his naked skin sliding over mine assaulting me like a battering ram.

"Stupid hormones, and stupid vampire." Muttering under my breath before I can stop myself, I stab my hands through the holes of the shirt, yanking it on angrily.

"What is your plan now, Francesca?" I know he hears me, but the fact that he chooses not to make a smartass comment is very telling. The casual tone of his voice even more so.

"How optimistic of you to think I actually have a plan." Blowing away the loose strands of hair that have fallen over my face, I focus on searching for an elastic band to secure it again. "I wasn't prepared to come back here to face a witch hunt. Stupidly, I thought we had averted a disaster by bringing you back and cutting the numbers of Roberti's goons." Finally turning to face him, my breath hitches at his smoldering gaze. "I know, very Panglossian of me, you don't have to say it."

"They are looking for ways to back you into a corner because that's the only way they can maintain control of the situation. You are a wild card." I hate that I take a step back as soon as he moves closer. Locking my knees, I force myself to stand still and ignore the drumbeat in my chest that's rocking my frame. "An unknown that is shaking the foundations of their rule."

"I love that everyone likes to pretend I wasn't thrown into this out of left field. It must be wonderful to live in this delusional world where Francesca has a notorious agenda to destroy the academy and everyone in it." The pain from the nails biting the skin of my palms is the only thing holding me back from screaming at him. It's not his fault this clusterfuck happened ... well not all his fault in any case.

"Did you?" I wobble slightly when one corner of his mouth kicks up in his familiar smirk.

"Seriously?" All the mushy feelings that were making me stupid when it comes to Zoltan evaporate with an almost audible hiss inside me. "You think I had some hidden agenda, too? How dare you!"

Spinning on my heel, I stomp to the door and yank it open. My skin prickles when he materializes behind me, his chest brushing my back. His palm slaps the wood, stopping my attempt to escape by leaving the gap too small to squeeze out of. Leaning firmly against me, he shoves it closed and tilts his face slightly, just enough for me to be aware of the fact that I can kiss him if I just turn my head his way. A fist tightens in my belly from his nearness.

"I know you don't, so don't use this as an excuse to run from me, Francesca. They are grasping at straws, and your behavior only proves their point, especially if you refuse the offer because anyone here would kill to get it. It's the only reason I didn't separate their heads from their shoulders in that hall. We must play this smart and see who is pulling their strings."

"If Roberti had any of them in his pocket, he wouldn't need a nobody to steal that book. They would've delivered it on a silver platter while we were busy chasing our tails." Catching myself leaning on his chest, I stiffen and straighten up. "Everything in me says they are working together but the facts don't match my gut feeling."

"Then we look for proof." He nuzzles my hair. "I'll be coming with you when you see your friend the mage."

"Like hell you are." Elbowing my way out of the cage he formed when he curved around me, I slam a hand on my hip. "Nobody is coming when I see Daren. I need him to speak freely, not worry if you will kill him the moment he opens his mouth."

"If you want him to live, I will be coming." He shouldn't look that hot with those blue eyes turned into slits and his jaw clenched, yet some dumb part inside me preens that he is jealous. Is he jealous though, or does he just want to make sure I'm not hiding anything from them? That's a very dangerous thought right now so I change the subject.

"And just for the record, I'm not running from you."

Lifting my chin, I stare down my nose at him, daring him to disagree.

His lips curve into a smile that triggers my fight or flight instinct.

"Yes, you are, Francesca Drake." Zoltan's voice purrs softly, and my heart speeds up, covering me in goosebumps. "But I do love a good hunt. Go ahead and run, female. I dare you."

So, I bolt out of his room.

Chapter Seven

My foot catches on something the moment I'm out the door. With a shriek, I throw my hands in front of me to soften the fall when I pitch forward, only succeeding to sprawl in the hallway like the outline of a body at a crime scene with my limbs in awkward angles. The air is pushed out of my lungs with a loud oomph, my chin and right side of my face throbbing from a numbing pain. When a weight settles on me, I groan. A large paw between my shoulder blades presses me down, and bursts of hot air are stirring the hair around my ear in short puffs.

My heart skips a beat.

A displeased growl vibrates from the panther who's pinning me in the hallway like some thief, and the jerk sits on my lower back leaving me at his mercy. Zoltan's barely-contained chuckle only adds insult to injury. It isn't how I want this day to start for sure. The whole plan in my head when I decide to literally run from the vampire does not involve a stubborn shifter sleeping in front of the closed door. Wisely, Zoltan does not offer me a hand up.

Pushing the feline off me, I roll to the side before jumping to my feet. Avoiding looking at both of them, I straighten my clothing, lift my chin up, and very carefully walk down the hall. Considering myself lucky that no one else witnesses this embarrassment, I go in search of Leo and Fenrir. They should be back by now with some information about Daren.

"They should be in the dining hall." At Zoltan's comment, I turn around instead of heading toward the hall to check Fenrir's room.

"Thank you," I tell him primly and I don't have to see him to feel his arrogant smile because I can feel it at the back of my head.

Just like I can feel eyes following our progression through the academy. They are prodding at me like accusing fingers, their hushed conversations like a cloud of bees vibrating my eardrums. My hands stray so I can wipe my sweaty palms off my pants but I catch myself and let them hang loosely at my sides. *Never show fear, Franky. Especially not now.* Repeating that in my head, I fasten my steps just enough to breeze through without jogging. I'm pissed that the two males are following behind me like shadows but I'd be lying if I said that it's not helping to keep my anxiety in check.

My feet falter slightly when I reach the fork where the hallway splits left for Soren's room and right towards the dining hall. Zoltan must've come to the same conclusion and figured out that I'd want to speak with the Fae at some point because I can feel his power surge when I think about stepping in the golden hall and leaving him behind. It's very tempting, I'm not going to lie, but I need to find out if I can see Daren and that's more important than my need to irk the Daywalker, so I turn right without too long of a hesitation. Without the tension in the air from the vamp, it's already easier to breathe.

Silas's son, with a handful of his friends, exits the dining hall just as I reach the entrance. His face tightens, pulling on the scar on his face and making me brace for a fight, or at least an insult. If looks could kill, I'd be dead many ways over, the venomous look in his eyes shocking me mute. I'm used to being eyed with wariness or even plain dislike, but I can't say I've ever felt anything like his hatred even from the hunters I've faced.

"Keep walking."

My head turns to Zoltan at his whispered words, but he is not talking to me. A deep growl comes from the panther's chest to punctuate the Daywalker's threat and he pins his ears to the back of his head, his upper lip curling over sharp teeth as long as my hand. The blood drains from Silas's son's face, leaving that scar stark against pale skin as he storms away from us, taking his friends with him.

"Let's go." Placing his large hand at the small of my back, Zoltan leads me inside the dining hall.

"I don't understand what that male's problem is." Wrestling my heartbeat under control, I let him guide me to the table where Fenrir and Leo are eating with not many others around.

"He is his father's son," is all the explanation I get and pretty much all that's needed. Silas has hated my guts from day one, and it's not a secret.

The Fae and the alpha stiffen when we reach them, their gazes going from me to Zoltan in question. The vampire nudges me to sit on one of the long sofas, plopping down next to me with a subtle shake of his head. I don't have it in me to call them out on the silent conversation going on right now, which is still unsettled by the hatred I faced a moment ago. Gnawing on the inside of my mouth, I look from Fenrir to Leo.

"Did you find Daren?" Zoltan shifts next to me, his thigh brushing against mine reminding me how close he is sitting.

"The mage has fire in him to be sure." Leo grins and, just like that, the knot in my stomach loosens. "I didn't think we'd need to give him a message from you so he'd hear us out."

"Leo learned the lesson when his tail was on fire and he was yelping out of the pub." Fenrir chuckles, then out right laughs when Leo glowers at him. "It was the highlight of my night."

"I bet it was," I tell him dryly, the Fae turning his breathtaking smile on me. "What did he say? He knows a way for me to go see him?"

"Fenrir." Zoltan arches an eyebrow at the Fae.

"Already done. No one can hear our conversation." Waving his graceful fingers, Fenrir dismisses Zoltan's concerns. "What do you take me for?"

"Emotions are running high right now, and we all make mistakes." The only apology Zoltan gives is a slight nod of his stupidly pretty head.

"You should know, huh." Unable to swallow it down, I throw the jab at him.

Leo snorts, covering it up with a cough.

Zoltan glares at him.

"The mage was not happy to hear what we had to say." Fenrir steers us back on track, plucking a piece of apple from his plate. "Told us you are a big girl and if you got yourself in trouble, you'd get out of it on your own." Stabbing the air with the fruit slice, he cocks his head to the side, his platinum hair sliding over his shoulder. "I find it very interesting that he wasn't worried about you at all. Especially since I saw that he cares the first time I spoke to you in his pub."

"Daren knows I can take care of myself." A smile blossoms on my face, warmth spreading through me that my friend has faith in me but turning to ice in my veins when Zoltan growls menacingly. "What the hell is your problem?"

"If he is your friend, he should be worried that your life is in danger, more so now than ever," he snaps at me, his lips pressing in a thin line.

"Him not being worried doesn't mean Daren doesn't care. It means he trusts that I can handle it. Unlike you." I would've moved away from him to sit in a chair but the panther is sprawled over my feet preventing me from moving. So, I just glare at Zoltan.

"She does have a point." I'm surprised Leo speaks up, but he definitely gets Zoltan's narrow-eyed gaze shot his way when he does. Fenrir, on the other hand, is nibbling the apple and watching the three of us with amusement dancing in his expression.

"You don't have anything to add to this insanity?" I wiggle in hopes to slide away from Zoltan, but he clamps a hand on my thigh and drags me back.

"No." Fenrir beams at Zoltan, lifting an eyebrow when the Daywalker stiffens. "It's fascinating to watch really. Better you than me, my friend." Saluting Zoltan with the leftover apple, he pops it in his mouth and chews it cheerfully.

"Daren." Pressing my fingers over my eyes hard enough to see bursts of light behind my closed eyelids, I blow out a breath. "Did he tell you how I can get out through the gates to see him?"

"As we suspected, since you are bound to the magic

holding this place up, you can't go past the gates to Sienna. Your friend confirmed what we knew as well." All the humor is gone when Leo speaks, rubbing the back of his neck. "We managed to get the mage to talk to us long enough, but no solution came from that. I almost forgot to give him your message but remembered it as we were leaving the pub." He exchanges a look with Fenrir that tells me absolutely nothing. "He said to meet him in the human realm tomorrow, wrote down an address on a napkin, and told us to never come back to his pub unless we want a fight."

"He can come to the portals to use them to go to the human realm?" Turning from Fenrir to Zoltan, my eyebrows crawl to my hairline. "I never thought of that until now. Do others use the portals we are protecting? I thought only those in the academy can use them."

My mind is racing from all this. If anyone in Sienna can use the portals, then we have no idea who is sneaking out and feeding information to the hunters. More troubling is the fact that anyone from the agency who may be working for Roberti can be going in and out, gaining access to us as well as the library.

"That's the thing," Leo cuts through my dazed thoughts. "He can't use these portals."

If I am not one-hundred percent sure that Zoltan will never hurt me, I may be running like crazy the second Leo finishes his sentence. A strong pulse of anger blasts from him, burning my skin like I have the sun itself sitting next to me. I can feel the fluid under my skin bubbling and blistering, but I'm frozen in place and unable to do anything about it. I know exactly how a moth feels when it finally reaches the flame.

"Zoltan." Fenrir lifts slightly off his seat, the Fae magic

swirling around him like a tornado and picking up the ends of his hair on a non-existent breeze. "Calm down." The Fae snarls, his blue eyes turning into bottomless black pits with white pupil.

As sudden as it starts, the pain and pressure disappear. I slump on the sofa as both Fenrir and Zoltan take deep breaths, rolling their shoulders to loosen up. That's when I notice the warm body pressing on my calves. Looking down at the panther, he is half crouched while leaning on my legs, one of my hands tangled in his fur. A green glow surrounds him, writhing like tendrils of smoke. Following them with my eyes, I realize they wrap around me too, forming a thin barrier with me and the shifter inside it.

"You good?" Fenrir's voice snaps my gaze to him. He is looking at Leo, who is still half lifted off his chair like he can't decide if he should sit back down.

"I need a second," the alpha growls more than he speaks, his face contorted between human and wolf. It's eerie to see him partially shifted with blood dripping from his nose. "Drake?" Leo glances at me with pain-filled eyes.

"I'm good." Scrubbing the back of my hand under my nose, I check to see if I'm bleeding as well. Nothing is smeared on my skin. "It's not my time of the month yet." My laugh is strained and I avoid looking at Zoltan.

"Tenebris protected her from the brunt of it." Fenrir eyes the panther thoughtfully as he finally lowers in his chair. "I wasn't aware he could share his powers like that with someone else."

"At least I know his name." I can hear a heartbeat in my mouth, and it makes my words shaky. Zoltan flicks a hand out and shoves the panther away from me, but the shifter only snarls in response as he nips him. "Is it safe to ask what that was all about?" I reach for Zoltan, placing my hand on his forearm to stop him from grabbing the feline.

"The only known portals to the human realm are the ones we are protecting behind our gates." Smoothing his hair away from his face, Fenrir crosses one ankle over a knee and leans back. "Which brings the question of how the mage will be using a portal, and if there is one somewhere in Sienna, how is it that we don't know about it."

"Sienna has no portals outside the gates." There is not a trace of doubt in Zoltan's voice. "The mage will be using one of ours."

"This is a bad thing how exactly?" My stomach growls like an angry dinosaur, and that turns all four sets of eyes on me. My face heats up like a stovetop, making me wish the ground will open to swallow me whole. "I need to speak to him away from here. Who cares how he will come to meet me as long as he comes?" Ignoring my embarrassment, I plow through with determination born of days going hungry in my younger days. Nothing to see here folks. The hunger will go away soon enough.

Raising my chin, I dare them to say something.

All three of them spring into motion, piling food on plates and shoving them in front of me. Scrubbing a hand over my face, I bite my tongue to stop myself from telling them I don't need food. I need answers. If I don't get them soon, hunger will be the least of my problems. With Roberti pissed that we killed a good chunk of his hunters and the Board plotting to screw me all the way to Sunday, an empty stomach is a good problem to have.

"How will I …" Zoltan uses my distraction to pop a piece of meat in my mouth, which shuts me up. Closing my mouth, I chew the morsel like an angry cow chomping on stubborn weeds, though I keep my eyes narrowed at him.

The asshole grins, waving another piece in my face.

Swallowing fast, I snatch his wrist and hold him back. "How will I find the address when I go through the portal?"

"I will take you there." Removing my hand, he presses the food to my lips until I take the offering.

"I will speak with Daren alone." The food is so delicious that saliva floods my mouth, dribbling through my lip when I speak with my mouth full. Suck it up jerk, I'll keep talking even if you stuff me like a bell pepper.

"You will speak with him alone." Inclining his head like a king from his throne at a peasant, he lifts a cube of cheese and holds it out for me. "I'll be close, but you can see the mage on your own."

"Wow, how very nice of you." I gush sarcastically before snatching the cheese from his fingers. "I can eat on my own, so no need to feed me." Grinning, I stuff the food in the panther's mouth, almost losing my hand in the process.

"So stubborn." Fenrir chuckles and returns to his apples. "It is set then. We will hold the perimeter while she tries to find …" He pauses, a slight frown forming a line on his forehead. "What is it exactly that you want to find, Hellion?"

"If Roberti is working with someone from Sienna, Daren will know about it." So, I don't have to look at the others, I focus on the fascinating plates of food in front of me. "I don't think it's a coincidence that the Board creates all this chaos right as we deal a blow to the hunters that's big enough to give us the upper hand. None of them knew it wasn't orchestrated."

"It'll be an easy back and forth." Leo is back in his human form but he looks tired, like he hasn't slept in weeks. "I'll have people watching the portals to see which one the mage will use. They won't stop him." He assures me when I open my mouth.

Zoltan pops cheese between my lips, and that pisses me off.

"Hunters are gathered on the other side on every portal." Astara comes rushing like a whirlwind, her hair tousled all around her face.

The cheese lodges in my throat, choking me.

Chapter Eight

"Roberti doesn't have to kill me. You almost did the job yourself," I rasp, my throat burning like I've had barbed wire for breakfast.

"Don't talk." Zoltan presses a glass of water to my lips, rubbing my back with his other hand. Tears are running in rivulets down my face.

"What have I missed?" Astara bounces on the opposite sofa, giving me an apologetic smile. "Sorry, Franky. I need to work on my delivery for next time."

"Let's hope there is no next time." Swiping at my blurry eyes, I sniff pitifully. "Geez, I really just kicked the bucket from a piece of cheese."

"That …"

"If you say that Daren had anything to do with this, I'm going to cut your throat while you sleep." I cut Leo off with a glare.

"…is very bad timing," the alpha finishes, slowly raising an eyebrow at me.

63

"So bloodthirsty." Fenrir cuts me a side glance, displeasure written all over his angelic face.

"She's magnificent." Smoothing a piece of hair behind my ear, Zoltan's gaze is burning a hole on the side of my face.

"You were feral a little over twenty-four hours ago. It doesn't sound like a compliment coming from you." Slapping his grabby hands away, I ignore Astara's knowing smile. "You think they'll breach the portals again?"

"They can't. None of them survived that were in the house where they had Zoltan." Fenrir leans forward placing his forearms over his thighs. "They couldn't get their hands on your blood and whatever Roberti has from before won't be enough to open every portal."

"Opening one is enough for us to have our hands full." Rubbing my neck gingerly, I hope the sting will go away soon so I don't sound like a smoker killing two packs a day. Smoking doesn't affect supernaturals, but I've heard enough of them on human television to know I sound exactly the same.

"Someone must've heard you talking to the mage."

I have no idea how Zoltan can do this. No matter what he says, there is so much conviction in it that you can't find it in you to doubt him. No wonder everyone here looks up to him and follows directions without a second thought. With the certainty coming out of him, even I will jump in the fire and burn to ashes if he tells me to do it. It's staggering to feel it the way I do right now.

"I was very careful." Fenrir frowns at his feet, confirming my thoughts that you can't doubt Zoltan. The Fae is trying to see how he could've slipped.

"I walked in alone first." Leo looks troubled. "It could've been something I said that triggered this."

"We are all missing the point here." A purr like an engine starts at my feet and I realize I've been rubbing the shifter under his chin. I snatch my hand back in dismay. "This just proves that Roberti has eyes and ears in Sienna."

"Or he is pissed that we whipped his ass and is planning to retaliate." Tilting her head, Astara shrugs a shoulder. "It's a possibility. He is a sore loser."

"The only thing he will lose is his head when he stops running like a coward." The panther perks up at Zoltan's menacing words.

I notice for the first time that we are the only ones in the dining hall. It's very strange to see the vast place empty. Cocooned in our bubble of silence so we are not overheard, I don't think the rest of them are aware. Leo is the first to lock his gaze on my face and turn around to see what has gotten my attention. The rest stop whatever they are talking about mid-sentence doing the same.

"The portals." Astara jumps up ready to run to the clearing, but I'm already shaking my head.

"Francesca?" Zoltan is watching me intently, his body coiled up and ready to spring.

I can't speak from the churning of my magic inside me, the force of it pressing on my bones like a living thing trying to burst out of an eggshell. Me being the eggshell in this case. Dizziness makes me sway where I'm sitting on the sofa, my vision blurring from the bright colors pulsing to life in my normal sight. The entity sharing my body is seething in rage, but I'm not able to understand the reason behind it because my bones bend to contain my powers, leaving me in excruciating pain.

"Ag obair còmhla, fuil drágon!" Fenrir snaps sounding very far away, but it's enough to clear my head. "You must

65

work together," he tells me while Zoltan bares his fangs at the Fae.

"Thank you." Gasping for breath, I latch onto Zoltan's arm so he doesn't attack Fenrir for yelling at me. "I thought I was going to split apart. Something is inside the academy."

Now that I know my skin is not going to be shred to ribbons, I can feel why the rage is bubbling in my veins. Someone dared to come uninvited to the land tied to my dragon blood and this thing inside me is pissed. It doesn't help matters that my anger and fear are coming off me in waves, fueling Zoltan and the others until all of them shed their humanity for the true predators they are.

Tenebris jumps on the table, sending plates of food flying all over the place and crashing on the floor. The panther's tail is flicking in agitation, his ears pinned to the back of his skull and his gaze locked on something across the room. All of us angle our bodies in the same direction, following the animal's instincts on a primal level.

That's when I see it.

The air ripples, thickening, swirling, and pulsing like a heartbeat in the middle of the dining hall. It shimmers with sparks flying like electrical outbursts, growing in size and density. A calm washes over me very different than the one I get when my heartbeat slows just as Zoltan slides forward and places himself between me and whatever is about to materialize inside the academy. I'm too busy trying to understand the feeling to be frustrated at his caveman tactics.

Fenrir, Leo, and Astara spread around just as I see Argoz running through the doors and screeching to a halt at the sight of the pulsing lights. The ghoul doesn't need explanations as he joins the rest, circling whatever is about to pop into existence. It all happens in a blink of an eye, but to me it feels like a day has passed, the absence of the anger rattling me inside weakening my knees. *Way to go Franky. Everyone is freaking out about how powerful you are, and you can't even keep yourself standing, you dumbass.* If the voice in my head had a physical body, I would've punched her in the uterus.

The shimmering forms into what resembles a body, limbs and a head taking shape from the sparking lights. His belly brushing the floor, the panther slinks closer with his tail lashing the air. My feet follow on their own behind him with Zoltan hot on my heels.

Everything happens at once.

Daren pops in front of us, his hair sticking out in all directions like he just walked through a hurricane, eyes darting wildly until he locks on me. Leo jumps him with Astara at the same time while Fenrir sends a blast of some freakish Fae shadows that wrap around all three of them. Tenebris sails through the air, joining the pile of bodies in the fray. I finally find my voice, somehow shaking off the shock of seeing my friends face in the middle of this place.

"No!" My shriek bounces around the empty space, echoing, but drowning in the grunts and snarls coming from the heap on the floor. "Stop!" Snatching Zoltan, I tug harshly on his arm because I can't find any words from the fear that Daren is already half eaten under the pile.

I sag, leaning on the vampire when he sends his mind fuck like a wave hammering everyone. All of them jump off Daren, moving fast to put enough distance between them so they aren't attacked when my friend gets up. *If he gets up.* But I shove that doubt away with everything in me. Only the panther doesn't have a care in the world as he chomps on Daren's arm like it's his personal buffet.

"Tenebris, that's Francesca's friend. The mage." Using

my distraction to his advantage, Zoltan gathers me in his arms, speaking as if he is exchanging pleasantries at a social gathering.

The panther's eyes open wide and lock on mine. I swear he looks chagrined. Very slowly and purposely, he opens his jaw, pushing Daren's bloody arm away from his teeth with his tongue. He even goes to great lengths to gag and cough, which makes me think he's about to cough up a hairball. All I can do is gape at the absurdity of the situation.

"We have a problem," Daren grunts, pushing off the floor with his good arm.

"Yes, we do." Fenrir is back to a royal Fae, staring the mage down his nose." Let's start with how you managed to portal yourself in here through the wards."

"Roberti has your mother." Ignoring the Fae, Daren watches me like I'm about to go into hysterics.

Everyone turns to look at me.

"This is excellent news." Excitement surges through me, but I stomp on it when they all look like I've lost my mind.

"He took her Franky." Daren takes a step toward me and Zoltan tightens his arms around my chest.

"Let her process the shock in her own time." Astara rushes to me, coming to hug me on the other side of Zoltan.

I'm the ham in a brother-sister sandwich.

Hysterical peals of laughter burst out of me.

"We will get her back, Drake," Leo growls, a fierce expression tightening the lines on his face.

"Oh, dear fates."— I howl harder and a stitch forms on my side— "you guys are serious."

"It's the shock," Astara murmurs, giving me a reassuring squeeze to let me know she's here for me. I love her for it but her concerns are not needed.

"Daren."—Knowing he is the only one that might

understand, I get myself somewhat under control— "it's my mother you are talking about. Have you met her?"

"Once." A familiar smile makes an appearance on his face. "But Roberti is insane. I had to tell you."

"I don't get it." Astara leans back, holding me at arm's length. "It's not shock, you really are laughing."

"They were estranged ..." Fenrir cocks his head, searching my face like you would look at an unfamiliar bug under a loop.

"I learned my fighting and mastered the weapons from my father." Wiping the tears from my eyes, I nudge Zoltan to release me with no results. "My attitude, the stubborn streak, and no patience for fools is all from my mother. Roberti will regret the day he took her under his roof. She's a tough cookie; she'll be fine until we get to her. If we are lucky, she'll drive him to hang himself just so he doesn't have to deal with her."

"She might be feral when we find her." Zoltan kisses the top of my head, reminding me of how I found him. "Good thing we have a cure for that."

"You think that's why the hunters are gathering around the portals? They think when I find out I'll run there mindless of the danger?" The vampire holding me in his arms as if someone might steal me away turns my insides to mush, so I lean on him and bask in his body being wrapped around me. *Just for a little while*, I lie to myself.

"It's as good a guess as any." We all look at Argoz when he speaks. "I was coming to ask for help when they told me what was going on with the portals. Those stationed on guard alerted the Board."

Daren stiffens visibly, and that gets my attention.

"You still need to tell us how you managed to portal

yourself past the wards, mage." Arms folded over his chest, Fenrir glares at Daren.

"Why does it matter? He is here." Detangling myself from Zoltan with great effort, I jump to the side to get away from him. The damn vampire is like Velcro. "We don't have to wait to talk until tomorrow."

"There are hunters on all portals." When I squint at Astara, she shrugs sheepishly.

"Good thing he portals himself then." I haven't finished the sentence when Zoltan yanks me to him, clamping on my upper arm in case I'm planning to bolt.

Greater males have shrunk from the death glare I give him, but he only narrows his eyes as if daring me to try. Okay, so I am, ready to bolt but the Daywalker doesn't need to know that. I'm still pissed he can read me so easily until I remember the link that opened between us when we exchanged blood in the shower. I've been broadcasting like a freaking radio station blaring every intention loud and clear to him. How did I forget that?

Kill me now. I'm so stupid.

"Well mage?" Fenrir hasn't looked away from Daren, but a muscle jumps in his jaw.

"Well this in unexpected." Hearing Silas speak from the entrance of the dining hall is like listening to someone scraping nails on a chalkboard. All three of the old jerks stand with various expressions on their faces. From disgust on Silas, disbelief on the shifter, to utter bewilderment on the mage.

"Daren?" The mage Board member steps forward, his chin hitting his chest in a comical fish out of water style.

"Father." Daren jerks his chin up as he glares at the mage.

My own chin hits the floor at my feet.

Chapter Nine

All sorts of things go through my head. Betrayal is loudest among them and it squeezes my heart like a fist. Zoltan turns into granite at my back when he hears the exchange, but I can't look away from Daren to placate the Daywalker. Instead of watching his father, my friend is keeping his eyes steady on my face as if waiting for my judgment.

No, not waiting for it. Expecting it.

The same way I always expect to be shunned or ostracized for being a half blood.

Despite knowing all this, I still lift my hand and reach for his arm. Dubiousness is like a living thing in the room with us, everyone's thoughts drowning in doubts and implications of being blindsided like this. From what I know of the mage Board member, I can't say I blame Daren for not advertising his bloodline. The same way he never held it against me when I shied away from speaking about mine.

He searches my eyes for a long moment before clenching his jaw and stepping closer, tugging the shirt up his forearm so I can touch him skin on skin. Tears prickle the corners of my eyes that I blink away, hoping beyond hope that he will not be just another person in a pile of others I've known most of my life that has manipulated me. Even while thinking it, deep down I don't believe it. At the moment, though, uncertainty is a luxury I can't afford. I need to be one-hundred percent certain he isn't a traitor. Everything he told me couldn't be a made-up fairytale just to get closer to me and for me to trust him, could it?

The grief hits me first, buckling my knees the second I touch him as his emotions pull inside of me. Zoltan snarls but doesn't move away from me, his arms the only thing keeping me standing. In an attempt to respect Daren's privacy, I do my best to block the blood connection between me and the Daywalker, but I know a lot of it passes through. The deep heavy breaths coming from Zoltan tell me as much. Maybe that's the only reason he doesn't attack the mage.

There is a mixture of everything, including fear, but no sign of manipulation or malice no matter how hard I pull, dragging everything he is hiding inside him into myself. A person with better morals than myself would've released him when they didn't find anything that would implicate him as a traitor. Convincing myself that I'm only doing it to be sure I can trust him, I dig inside the fear he feels. Daren's muscles twitch under my fingers, his hand clenching at my prodding even though he doesn't pull away. Not at first.

With a gasp, I jerk away from him and cradle my hand to my chest. Zoltan tilts his body and hides me from Daren, but I can't look away from my friend. I think he fears the Daywalkers, or even me to some degree maybe. But the unease eating a hole inside him comes from his father. The problem is I can't be sure if it's because he suspects the mage Board member of betraying us or if he is afraid that his father will give away his own secrets. I glance at Zoltan to see if he got a feel of any of it, but his intent gaze is burning with concern and something I'm too chicken shit to name right now.

"Can we hear what is going on, or are you planning to leave us in the dark?" Argoz tugs on the collar of his shirt, turning at each of us one at a time.

I don't want to share anything in front of the old jerks, so I reach for my friend. Daren's shoulders visibly slump, and he takes my fingers in a bruising grip to allow me to pull him closer to me and Zoltan. That is enough for the rest of our group to move in and form a tightly-knit circle facing the Board, while Argoz shifts restlessly between us.

"What is the meaning of this charade?" Silas glowers at us, gulping and taking a step back when the panther growls deep and low in his chest.

"What are you doing here Daren?" The mage is over his shock, the electricity swirling around his long, bony fingers again.

"I'm visiting a friend. Last time I checked that wasn't against the rules." Daren throws his shoulders back, looking like the badass mage I've always known him to be.

"A friend." Silas looks at me with his mouth twisted in disgust.

"Yes, me," Fenrir chirps from behind me and I get whiplash from how fast my head snaps in his direction.

"No one saw him go through the gates." The shifter tucks his chin to his chest, puffing up his chest in aggression and ignoring Silas and his remarks. "We have hunters congregating around us like fleas. How did you get here?"

"He used the portal," Daren's father says dismissively like it's a common thing for people to open gateways wherever they like. "He's been doing that since he started walking."

Daren gives him a wide smile, more a baring of teeth than anything else.

"Why are you here?" Zoltan obviously had enough of watching things unfold because he steps away from me to square off with the old jerks. I grab the back of his shirt, fisting it as if that will hold him back if he decides to attack the idiots glaring at us.

Leo coughs, and Astara snickers next to him.

"We need to know what transpired in the human realm to bring them nipping at our heels." Silas sneers, but he doesn't look at Zoltan.

"You should've asked that first instead of creating chaos when we returned." To anyone else, it'll sound like Zoltan is having a reasonable discussion. The short hairs on my neck and arms lift at attention at the undercurrent of power punching each of his words.

"Zoltan, we can discuss this in a calm manner ..." Argoz gulps, taking a few steps back and staggering when Zoltan turns his head very slowly to look at him. "We need to work together," the ghoul whispers miserably under his breath.

Zoltan watches Argoz, his eyes unblinking.

It's unnerving.

"Never mind." Throwing his arms in the air, Argoz shuffles out of the dining hall giving a wide berth to the Board members.

One down, three to go.

"None of this was a problem—" Silas starts but I've had enough of his shit.

"Yeah, yeah we know. None of it was until I got here. We heard you the first hundred times. Come up with something new because this is getting old." Releasing Zoltan's shirt, I step next to him with my hands propped on my hips. "The fact that you had Cassius, his daughter, and Alexius working with Roberti behind your back is a minor detail, right? We should also ignore all the deaths in Sienna too because those are irrelevant. Everything that matters to you is between these walls, so here we are. Maybe now we will matter enough for you to pull your heads out of your assess and find a solution to the problem." Silas scrunches up his face in rage, so I grin at him. "It's uncomfortable when the fire is under your ass instead of someone else's, isn't it?"

I can feel Zoltan's gaze on the side of my head, so I turn to him. My heart skips a beat at the potency in the blue orbs glued to my face. The slight twitch of the corner of his mouth sends my insides somersaulting before butterflies erupt in my belly. Everything around me fades away, leaving me snarled in the fervency of the Daywalker. My body sways towards him like a moon in orbit of a planet. I'm unable to pull away. Astara stabs a finger between my ribs, jerking me out of the trance. Silas is talking but I missed half of it.

"Say what now?" I blink fast to clear the cotton that replaced my brain when I catch the words "tricking Soren" and "Roberti's pawn."

"You infiltrated this academy and turned everything on its head, Ms. Drake. You can't tell me your appearance here when the portals are failing or being breached is a coincidence." The shifter huffs indignantly at me. "You may use your wiles on the younger males so they can't see through your deceit, but we are members of the Board for good reason. You cannot fool us."

"By that account, you shouldn't want her as part of the guild." Fenrir is practically gloating right now. "We wouldn't want someone using their wiles in our inner circle. Too many younger males to corrupt."

I believe Leo is about to cough out a lung.

"Now wait a minute." The shifter Board member shrivels under Silas's menace. "What we are saying is that was our main concern and will stay as such until the oath is given." Daren grabs my arm in a tight grip, and I have to bite the inside of my mouth so I don't scream in pain. "The sooner that is done and we know we have nothing to worry about, the sooner we can put our efforts in ridding ourselves of the vermin. The academy is first and foremost, and everything else comes second."

"Including waking—" I yelp, clamping my mouth shut when Astara tears out a handful of my hair.

"Waking what, Ms. Drake." The savagery brightening Silas's gaze douses the anger that almost makes me blurt out that we know Roberti is planning on waking up the Titans.

"Soren." Schooling my face to look as clueless as I can, I blink stupidly at his glower.

"I'm tired of this useless conversation." Turning his back to the old jerks, Zoltan dismisses them like they are some regular nobodies. "I got hungry from all the stupidity I heard." His eyes flick to my neck and I clamp my thighs in reaction. The perpetual smirk makes an appearance on his handsome face. "Unless you have some useful information to share, I suggest you go deal with your hunter problem. We as younger males will make sure Ms. Drake doesn't leave the academy or wander around unescorted."

With a hand on my lower back, he guides me to the table that looks like toddlers had a temper tantrum around it. There are broken dishes and shattered glasses all around it with food half stomped on and half whole sprinkled in the mess. Tenebris leads the way, nudging the vegetables away but chomping down on whatever meat is in front of his face. Skirting a puddle of what looks like juice, Zoltan lowers himself onto the sofa and pulls me down with him.

Daren debates for just a second before coming to sit on my other side. Puffing my cheeks, I release a long, deep breath bumping my shoulder on his in gratitude that he doesn't hold my mistrust against me. Pretending we don't see the old jerks still lingering at the doorway, Leo and Fenrir drag in some untouched plates set on the other tables. Zoltan starts eating like he's been starving for weeks, which in reality he might've been apart from the blood he took from me. I'm pretty sure Roberti didn't have catering set up for his prisoners.

Not daring to look directly at the Board members, I steal glances through my lashes while I pretend I'm listening to the meaningless chatter between Fenrir and Daren. The two of them are acting like BFFs, the lie thick enough you can cut it with a blade. When they slap each other's shoulders, I roll my eyes at how fake it looks. Thankfully the old jerks get tired of staring at the idiocy, so they spin on their heels and leave the dining hall.

We all deflate the second they vacate the space.

"You are not taking any oaths." Daren turns on me, making me jump off the sofa.

"I like him already." Astara gives the mage a smile to keep him awake for a month.

Leo snarls something under his breath but pretends it isn't him when we all look at him in surprise. I flick between the two of them, not for the first time wondering if there is something going on I'm not aware of. I'm oblivious to things like that, so I won't be surprised if I miss it. I let Fenrir explain everything that happened after we returned with Zoltan to Daren, watching my friend's reaction closely.

He hears it all, leaning back and staring at his hands. I look at them too, at the black ink displayed so proudly where the pure bloods have marked him as a traitor for daring to love a half blood, and it tightens my chest.

"You see why I have to do it, don't you?" I search his face, not knowing what I'm looking for. "I can't stop thinking about what Roberti said when they breached the portals. Everyone is loathing the vampires because they feel like they are below them. I didn't do anything on purpose, but my actions gave them hope. If I take that away, I won't be able to live with it."

"No matter the consequences?" Daren's question has Zoltan pausing with a fork full of food mid-air.

"It can't be worse than what I've had to deal with up to this point."

I wish I knew how wrong I was.

Chapter Ten

"I should've known you had something to do with all the insanity happening in Sienna lately." Shaking his head, Daren rubs a hand over his face before ruffling his hair with short, agitated moves.

"Excuse me?" Acid burns my mouth from his accusation. I want to speak with him because I think I'll get information, but that's not all. I want the support as well. My hopes go down the drain with his clenched jaw and flaring nostrils.

"Take it easy there, Franky." With a heavy sigh, he reaches for my upper arm, hesitating an inch from touching me. "I'm not blaming you for anything. It's been long overdue, but if anyone was going to turn everything on its nose, I should've known it'd be you." His hand falls limply on his thigh but a fond smile tilts the corners of his mouth. "You never were one to do things in a subtle way. More like an elephant dashing through a house of glass."

"He does have a point, Hellion." Fenrir chuckles but Zoltan's snort is what irks me more.

"Whatever." Huffing, I slump back on the sofa, gnawing on my mouth. "As glad as I am to see you, Daren, I wanted to talk away from this place." Zoltan rumbles deep in his chest, but I shut him up with a sharp look turned his way. "The old jerks just proved my point that you can't say anything around here without someone overhearing it. It'll be nice for a change to figure shit out without everyone going for our heads, don't you think?"

"She does have a point, Zoltan." Gathering his hair and tying it back with a sharp snap of the elastic band, Fenrir's lips form a tight white line. "Roberti pushed the first piece by sending her inside our gates. It's a domino effect we are dealing with and it's going down faster than we can keep up. The only question is: who will reach the end before the last piece drops."

"What is it with you and board games, Fae?" Frowning at him, I brush my sweaty palms on my pants because, as infuriating as he is, he does make a good argument.

"Strategy." When my eyebrows crawl up my forehead, Leo gives Fenrir a smartass smirk. "Every Fae I've ever known loves their strategy. It's what draws them to board games to fill their time." The alpha looks as smug as ever.

"Francesca is not going anywhere with the mage, alone or otherwise, until we address the problem all of you are willing to ignore." Pushing the now empty plate away with a cluttering of porcelain on wood, Zoltan turns his intense gaze on Daren. "You are Solomon's son."

"And?" I flinch away when Daren's face scrunches in anger, his magic sparking like fireworks.

"Too convenient at times like this if you ask me."

Throwing an arm over the back of the sofa, Zoltan angles his body to face my friend, curling around me in the process. All my nerve endings tingle from his nearness and I catch myself leaning into his chest. Straightening up with a jerk, I pretend I don't see his lips twitch even when his focus is entirely on Daren. The vampire is seriously too cunning for his own good while accusing me of the same thing. No one misses the possessive way Zoltan places a hand on my thigh, his fingers tracing patterns absentmindedly and sending my insides into a frenzy.

Although nothing he does is absentminded.

"I haven't seen or spoken to my father in a very long time. When I found out Francesca's mother was taken, I feared she would do something rash so I came to stop her. I wouldn't have come face to face with him anytime soon otherwise." Daren is watching Zoltan's hand with a slight crease between his eyebrows. His eyes move slowly up until they lock on mine. "I think Franky is right. A conversation is long overdue."

"We should trust your word for it, I take it." The Sahara has nothing on the dryness of Zoltan's words. I can't think straight from his touch, so I slap his hand away.

"We need to talk outside of this place. Are you all deaf?" Wiggling away from the two males, I jump to my feet. "We are wasting time bickering here when everyone can say what they think *outside* of the academy."

"Hunters are clustered at each portal, Franky." Astara climbs to her feet as well. "It'll be interesting going through them just to talk with Fenrir being able to ward us here."

"Daren can open portals." Flicking a hand at the mage, I squeeze my way past Zoltan's long legs just to get away from him.

"Convenient," the Daywalker says nonchalantly, lifting to his over six-feet height and following behind me like a shadow.

Spinning on my heel, I throw both hands in front of me

and halt his progress. Zoltan stops with a glare. "Stop. See this?" Turning in a circle with both arms stretched out in front of me, I do my best not to scream. "It's called a personal bubble. Respect that, you ... you ... argh!" I'm vibrating in frustration and can't think of what to call him, so I end up growling like an idiot. There is a lot of choking, coughing, and snorting from the others, but I don't look away from him.

"I don't trust him." Folding his arms over his chest and bunching the fabric of the shirt around his biceps, Zoltan stares me down with a stubborn lift of his chin.

"Congratu-fuckin-lation! I don't trust anyone." Scratching my arm in anger, I can feel skin filling up the space under my nails where I'm leaving red gouges in it. "Now that we have this out in the open, we need to move. I have no doubt the Board will find a reason why I should do that stupid oath sooner rather than later, so I'd like to have a plan before that happens if you don't mind."

Ignoring my comment about personal space, Zoltan takes my hand in his strong fingers, stopping me from mutilating myself. Maybe he has no idea what personal space means? Watching his thumb scrape over the back of my hand as if it's a snake that will bite me, my head jerks up when Daren laughs out loud. The mage has his head thrown back and he is pressing a hand over his chest.

"What's so funny?" Astara takes a surprised step back when I snarl like a feral beast.

"Only you, Franky." Daren howls louder, slapping his thigh. "I was worried they were manipulating you or threatening you in some way, so I wasn't sure if I wanted to portal everyone." Snickering and chortling, he pushes to his feet. "I should've known none of them stand a chance against you and the chaos that follows you everywhere, Daywalkers or not."

"Oh yeah." Leo snorts, joining Daren in some stupid male solidarity. "She had them all turned on their heads in the first five minutes she stepped foot here. I'm surprised none of the Board has had an aneurism yet."

"Ha ha, very funny. Let's see if you'll still be laughing after we tell you everything." Stabbing the air with a finger at Daren's face, I yank my other hand out of Zoltan's where he is still holding it hostage. "Come on, click your shoes three times and take us away, Dorothy."

"You know what she is talking about?" Leo turns to Fenrir.

"Some human television stuff, I'm sure." The Fae twists his mouth like he tasted something sour.

"I want to come wherever you are going." Argoz's voice floats from the doorway.

"I thought you had us warded so no one could hear our conversation." I glare at Fenrir.

"He didn't hear anything." The Fae looks insulted, but I don't care. I've had enough frustration for one day and today has barely started.

"I've made a lot of mistakes only because everyone is keeping vital information from me." The ghoul moves further inside the dining hall, the collar of his shirt gaping almost down to his navel by this point. He really needs to stop tugging on it. I'm starting to think he has more anxiety issues than me. "Everything I've known is falling apart. Don't keep me out of it. I can help."

"Let him come." At Fenrir's murmured agreement, Zoltan grabs my upper arm and propels me out of the room. "I need to get something from my room, and Francesca is coming with me."

"Francesca can walk on her own, thank you very much." Yanking on my arm, I'm practically jogging to keep up with his long strides, but that doesn't make him let me go. "Why do I need to come anyway? You know where your room is."

Argoz gives us a passing glance when we storm past him, but he rushes to join the others when the jerk next to me nods sharply at him. The ghoul looked like a lost puppy but now there is determination bordering on frantic excitement painting his features. I hope Zoltan knows what he is doing, because I haven't had a chance to form any type of opinion about Argoz. He is just there, popping up at random times. It's enough to be aware of his presence, but nothing more. Seeing him with the old idiots when they attacked our group at the portals didn't win him any points, either.

"Please tell me someone told her who he is." There is a hint of fear in Daren's voice, and it sounds far away by the time we reach the entrance of the dining hall. "She knows who Zoltan is, right?"

"I don't think she does." Fenrir chuckles, his words loaded with amusement.

"Even Daren thinks you are a bogeymen," I huff out when we turn down the hall. "It's all that one-word wonder personality you have going on."

"I think Myst is rubbing off on you." Zoltan flicks his gaze at me but doesn't slow down. "And not in a flattering way."

"She is onto something by staying away from you lot, I'll tell you that much." Finally freeing my arm because I don't want to admit he actually decided to release his grip, I rub at it. "Why did you need me to have your back? That's why you dragged me with you right?" Flicking a hand in his face when he opens his mouth, I narrow my eyes at him. "The next words coming out of your mouth better be, 'yes Francesca, I needed backup,' because if that's not it I'm going to be pissed."

"We can't leave it behind if all of us are going through a portal." My mouth forms an O at that. The book is in Zoltan's room. It's smart thinking to take it with us in case someone decides to break in and search for it. With everything going on, I forgot about the cursed thing. Okay, so he did need backup. A smile curls my mouth.

"I took you with me because the mage can't snatch you away if I'm near." Zoltan kills any warm fuzzies that start in my chest.

"You are an asshole. I hope you know that."

"So you've told me once … or twice." That corner of his mouth twitches again, and my palm is itching to slap his smirk away.

"Daren is in no way working with the Board or with Roberti." Remembering the grief that came off him, I rub a fist between my breasts. "If you knew his story, you'd know I'm right."

"Why don't you tell me." With a hand on the small of my back, he veers me left across the wide space of the academy's foyer.

"It's not my story to tell." I swallow the lump in my throat. "You felt some of what he is feeling through the blood bond, no?" I shouldn't have mentioned the bond.

It's not a normal thing for a half blood, this feeling of connecting he forged between us. Yes, I can feel the presence of anyone if I take their blood, but this is different. Ever since it happened, I've been so freaked out that I'm blocking it as much as I can. Is it the same for him? I don't dare dissect it long enough to figure out. And now I blurt it out like some idiot.

Zoltan nods slowly, thoughtfully, unaware of my inner turmoil.

"That was some very strong grief, indeed." My heart punches my ribs hard before hammering wildly. "It doesn't say he can be trusted." Shadows dance around his face, the light of the moon coming through the windows we are passing sharpening his cheekbones. "I'm not taking any chances when it comes to you, Francesca." Luckily, we reach the door to his room and I don't have to comment on that.

"Go get the cursed thing." Crossing my arms, I lean on the wall.

Zoltan stops with his hand on the door handle, his gaze searching my face for a long moment. Not looking away, I stare at him unblinking but inside I'm a mess. I hope he can't see how his last words affected me. Not because I need someone to protect me, but because of how everything inside me melts and turns to mush knowing someone is willing to try. His eyelids lower slightly and I can tell he wants to say more, but thankfully he opens the door and disappears inside. Releasing a deep breath, I sag on the wall. *What the hell are you doing Franky,* I ask myself, but I have no answer. When it comes to the Daywalker, I'm drifting like a speck of dust in the air with nothing to anchor me to reality. The one where me and him can be nothing but a passing thing.

"I have it." Zoltan walks out closing the door behind him.

"Great." He gives me a startled look at my chirpiness. "Let's go." The words rush out of me as I bolt down the hallway.

Initiated

I have no idea if I'm running from him, or from myself.

Chapter Eleven

"Take the rest of them first." Zoltan glares at Daren while holding me by the arm. "Francesca and I can go with you last."

Praying for patience, I nod at the mage because we will stay here for days if we argue with Zoltan. The Daywalker made it abundantly clear that we're doing things his way or we can take the highway. Daren looks between us with amusement, but it evaporates when Zoltan growls. The panther, who by some miracle doesn't follow me when we retrieve the book, is not helping either when he shoulders his way between us, plopping in front of me. Typical cat, no matter the size.

I watch in fascination when Daren glides his hands in the air and the space in front of him starts swirling and shimmering like a soap bubble in the sun. Astara, Leo, Fenrir, and Argoz gather behind him, watching each flick of his fingers or twist of his wrists with rapt attention. I'd be lying if I said I don't find it amazing. I mean the mage is literally ripping an opening in time and space right before our eyes. Until he popped inside the academy out of thin air, I thought portals were some anomaly connecting us to the humans. Daren just proved how wrong I've been.

"Where are we going?" Leo shifts from foot to foot, excitement making him practically vibrate in place. Astara elbows him to shut him up because he is disturbing the mage.

"I don't know about you, but I would like to step out on the other side with all my body parts in the right places," she hisses at the alpha.

"I have a house in the human realm and it's secluded. It'll be safe to speak there," Daren says low under his breath, not taking his eyes away from the opening portal or pausing in his movements.

The ground under my feet thumps slightly, but none of the others react. My power lurches in my chest, alerting me that something isn't right. Just like when Daren appeared earlier. The portal snaps open and the earth on which the academy stands shudders like it's cold. Not for the first time, I wonder if the magic protecting this place is a sentient entity we know nothing about.

"Go ahead." Daren shifts slightly, urging the others to go through.

"Here goes nothing."

Astara squares her shoulders and strides through it without a second glance. Leo is right on her heels, barreling through with a curse sounding like "damn stubborn females," but I can't be sure. Fenrir grabs Argoz by the back of his neck, propelling him ahead as he walks through as well.

"I'll be back in one second." Daren throws the words over his shoulder and steps through.

Without overthinking it too much I lurch my body

forward, tugging Zoltan's hand off my arm. As I knew they would, both the vampire and the panther jump at the portal, disappearing through it before it snaps closed, which leaves only me and Daren left standing in the middle of the empty dining hall.

"You really have a death wish." Daren snorts and scratches his head.

"Fuck!" Sucking in a deep breath, I fill my lungs to bursting and hold the air in. "He is going to kill me for this." Blowing the breath out, a hysterical giggle bubbles out of me.

"Care to tell me why we pissed off the most dangerous Daywalker that ever walked the worlds?" Daren's green eyes sparkle with mischief. Slapping his hands together, he rubs them harshly. "You never make life boring, Franky."

"It's Zoltan, he'll get over it." Waving his worry away, I push the spike of fear that passes through me to the back of my mind. "We need to make a pit stop before we join them."

"I'm not a taxi, Drake." There is no bite in his comment, but his eyes narrow on me.

"I'll owe you for this. I need to stop at my apartment, but I can't leave through the gates." Daren's eyebrows snap in a sharp V over his eyes but I rush ahead to convince him. "I just need one minute, two tops, and we will join them. Please, Daren."

'Why can't you leave through the gates?" The mage grabs my shoulders to stop me, bouncing on my toes in his urgency.

"I kinda die if I try to leave the academy," I mumble before the rest comes out in one breath. "If I kick the bucket, you can bring me back. It took you less than a second to return just now. Let's go." Daren jerks back like I've punched him.

"You die?" His eyes are about to pop out of their sockets, and I deflate.

"Listen, it's a long story and I promise I'll tell you everything later. The longer Zoltan waits for us to show up the more furious he will be." Chewing on my lip, I eye Daren. "Your house might get some redecorating. But anyway, since you are creating the portal, I think I'll be fine. You can even hold onto me the entire time if you like. I'm not doing anything stupid; I just need to get something."

A muscle is twitching in Daren's jaw and tiny flames are bursting in puffs around his clenched fists. "They are holding you here against your will." His face fills with darkness like a stormy cloud.

"What? No." It's my turn to be taken aback. With a groan, I cover my face with both hands. "Maybe at first," Daren hisses angrily so I pick at him through my fingers. "Like five minutes, give or take."

"Are you listening to yourself Drake?" The mage paces in front of me wearing a hole into the floor. "Do you know how insane that sounds?"

"At the time, I didn't know the academy was where I needed to be Daren." Dropping my arms, I glare at him. "Don't you see what's going on? You'd rather not know and leave the faith of Sienna in the useless hands of the Board? Or would you rather be in the thick of it where you actually have a say?" Not waiting for an answer, I shove a finger in his face. "I didn't think so."

"I see Zoltan's hands are more capable." He shuts his mouth with an audible snap. "I didn't mean that."

"Who I fuck is none of your business. The faith of

many lives is at stake here, so are you going to take me to Sienna or not?"

"I'll take you, but you better not die on me, Franky. I'm not dealing with that Daywalker on my own, am I clear?"

"Crystal." His hands are already moving so I don't argue anymore.

"You must be the dumbest female I've ever met if you think what's going on with that vampire is as simple as scratching an itch." Shaking his head like he can't believe my stupidity, Daren snorts incredulously.

"That's what it *was*. It's all in the past now." Staring him down my nose, I dare the mage to keep talking. Rattling around my ribcage, my heart is erratic, though on the outside I'm as calm as a cucumber.

"Keep telling yourself that." Pursing his lips, Daren can't even stop the snicker coming out of him.

"Just open the damn portal."

Grinding my teeth, I bite hard on my tongue to stop the idiotic butterflies that are bursting in my lower belly. The mage is too optimistic thinking everyone can find love just like he did. Didn't he learn a lesson when his female was killed? Unless he wishes all of us to suffer a loss like that, he can't possibly encourage this insanity. My eyes lock on the back of his hand where the black ink is stamped. I wonder if he will go through with it again if he can go back in time. Was it worth it? The question sits on the tip of my tongue, so I bite it until blood fills my mouth.

"Okay, Franky." Blowing out a breath, Daren has beads of sweat gathering around his hairline and above his upper lip. "I'll hold it open as long as I can so we don't waste time opening a new portal. You better be fast, or I'll have to fully step through and waste a few minutes to create another gateway directly to the human realm. If you are dying it might be a little tricky to concentrate. Never mind the fact that I'll bring you back just so I can kill you myself."

"You can do that?"

"Are you planning on dying?" At my frown, he shakes his head. "I can't, but I will definitely try if you don't stay breathing." He grins at me, but it's strained.

"Right." Blowing out a breath, I inch closer to the shimmering portal. "We will be in and out."

Bracing for the nausea that slaps me every time I walk through one of these damn things, I blindly step through, my face scrunched up stupidly. My foot hits something hard and sends me spinning, so I sidestep around it and grab onto soft fabric in hopes to stay standing. My eyes snap open and I blink fast to clear my vision so I can see my apartment, which is partly covered in shadows where the moon is not penetrating the darkness in front of me. The fact that I'm not curled on the floor fighting for breath makes me grin.

"Still alive," I call out to Daren, hoping he can hear me through the portal.

Not wasting time, I rush to my bedroom and yank the door open with too much force. It crashes against the opposite wall but I'm already tugging the mattress off the bad frame. My fingers curl around the headboard at the same time as claws dig into my neck, cutting off my air supply.

"I knew you'd eventually come here." Someone snarls in my ear, his rancid breath making me gag. "It was just a matter of time."

Dark spots dance at the corners of my eyes so I lift my leg, slamming the heel of my boot on his foot as hard as I can. The asshole roars in pain but his damn claws tighten around my neck instead of releasing me. Kicking, clawing, and scratching doesn't work either and hysterical laughter bubbles inside me. *Here lies Francesca: she fought demigods, hunters, and poisons just to be killed by a burglar,* my mind supplies my eulogy. The person killing me screams, bursting my eardrum before releasing my throat. Falling on all fours, I gulp air and cough as tears stream down my face, blurring the bedroom.

"Never a dull moment," Daren says from somewhere behind me and I see him kicking a body burnt to a crisp when I look over my shoulder. "At least you are not dying from being in Sienna. Hurry up and get what you need until I open a new portal, or I'll leave you behind."

Nodding jerkily, I pull the bed frame aside with shaky arms. My fingers are trembling while I fumble with the ridges between the planks on the floor. I miss it three times before finally catching the tiny gap and digging my nails into it. I don't open this hidden compartment often, so it takes a lot of effort and cursing until the part of the plank pops off. Scraping the shit out of my hand, I catch the cloth bag between my fingers and gingerly pull it out. With a sharp tug, I unravel the knot on the little bag, flipping it so the rock, which is the size of my thumbnail and sports a brass chain, drops into the center of my palm.

Closing my fist, I breathe in slowly. No one has been here, or if they had they didn't find the one thing my father gave me the last birthday he was alive. Swallowing the lump in my throat, I shove my hand inside the gaping hole again and pull out the flat leather holster I keep in it. Feeling the bumps of the blades neatly placed inside settles my nerves. The day I step into the academy is the day I lose everything that was mine. But it's time Roberti and those hunters face Francesca Drake in her style.

"Ready?" Daren sounds like he is about to faint, so I jump up.

"Yup, let's go." Hugging the necklace and the daggers to my chest, I face the mage.

"You look like the cat that ate the canary." Daren looks at what I'm holding suspiciously. "What's that?"

"Just some old friends I'd like to introduce to Roberti." Tucking my free arm around his, I turn us to face the portal. "Now we go to the human realm."

"I'll pretend I fainted until you calm the Daywalker." I burst out laughing when I see his serious face. "Like hell I'm going to deal with Zoltan for you."

"I got this; you have nothing to worry about." Still chuckling, I tug him through the portal.

The second I step through, I'm lifted off the ground and Daren drops on the floor unconscious, a black panther holding his neck between razor sharp teeth.

Chapter Twelve

"Stop!"

My shriek echoes around an open field surrounded on three sides by thick forests, the tall evergreens swaying sharply from the stormy weather. The one side not having trees is actually a humongous house very much like a wooden lodge standing three stories tall and protecting us from the sharp sting of the angry wind. Kicking my feet, I force Zoltan to put me down, although he is not releasing me. With his face twisted in a grimace, the vampire has his furious burning gaze locked on Daren, while I fight with my hair that's slapping my face.

"I'll kill him," Zoltan snarls, and the noise only riles up the panther, who is growling without even a pause to take a breath.

"He only did what I forced him to do, Zoltan." Yanking on his stiff arm, I try to get his attention. "I had to get this from my apartment." Waving the leather satchel in his face, I step between him and a still-unconscious Daren. Zoltan moves slightly to the side to keep an eye on the mage, which pisses me off. Since nothing is working, I sigh.

And punch him in the face.

"Francesca." I almost laugh at the shock in his deep voice, but I choke it down when his eyes narrow at me.

"There you are." Tugging on my shirt to straighten it up, I beam at him. "As I was saying, I had to take this so he did what I asked." Zoltan's gaze flicks to the leather satchel before returning to my face.

Silence stretches between us as thick as molasses, making it hard to breathe. The wind is still slapping my hair all over my face before lifting it around my head in chunks of dancing strands. I can see that Zoltan is fighting to gain control, his chest rising and falling in fast succession as the air whistles through his flared nostrils. Guilt stabs me in the chest since I scared him with my impulsiveness, but I shove it away fast. If I told him what I wanted to do he would've never agreed. The knot in my chest loosens when he lifts his hand to my face. Until his fingers brush my neck and he brings them between our faces covered in blood. Shit, I forgot the asshole that almost choked me to death.

"That was not Daren." I rush to assure the Daywalker, who's face is darkening in rage every time I blink. "He actually saved me."

Zoltan snarls.

"Okay I'm screwing this up big time." Blowing out a breath, my mind whirls with how to explain this without killing Daren in the process.

"It was a hunter," Daren rasps from behind me and Zoltan's fangs lengthen again.

"Keep your mouth shut." Hissing at the mage, I grab Zoltan's face to keep his attention on me. Then Daren's words penetrate the fog in my head. "A hunter?"

Whirling around, I lose my balance and Zoltan's hand latches onto me to stop me from falling. Maybe I should sway drunkenly to stop the Daywalker from attacking the mage. That's one way to calm the testosterone blasting me from all sides.

"A hunter." Still with his neck in the panther's mouth, Daren's eyes are locked on Zoltan over my shoulder. "A mutated hunter at that."

"The claws." A shiver crawls up my spine. "I thought it was a shifter or a demon."

Zoltan nods at the panther and the shifter releases Daren, stepping away. Rubbing at his neck, the mage pushes off the ground, eyeing me with an expression that makes me gulp air. My friend has never looked at me like that since I've known him.

"You are more trouble than you're worth." Daren lifts both hands in surrender when the panther bristles and bares his teeth at him. "I'm just saying. I didn't live this long to die without taking at least some of them with me."

"How are hunters getting in Sienna without using our portals?" Ignoring his comments, I look at Zoltan over my shoulder. "Are there others that can open portals like Daren?"

"No." Zoltan glares at the mage. Lo and behold, the one-word wonder is back.

"Yes, there is." Brushing leaves and dirt off his clothing, Daren walks away from us, heading for the house with a purpose. "I just didn't know he was still alive."

"Care to elaborate." Hurrying after him, I almost trip over the panther when he bumps into my leg and hip. The damn thing is silent death when he moves.

"I know of only one other mage that can open portals the way I do." Daren throws over his shoulder, reaching for the large entrance door of the house. "My uncle that I was told died long before I was born."

"So, Solomon is involved with Roberti." My body trembles at the menace in Zoltan's words.

"Not necessarily." Holding the door open for us, Daren waves his hand to hurry us along.

I don't have the luxury of enjoying the calm feeling Daren's house blankets us in. I'm aware that the foyer is open and wide with a large staircase curving all the way to the top on one side. Tall ceilings are crisscrossed with wooden beams, carriage wheels holding candles swaying above our heads like chandeliers. Sand-colored tiles cover the floor, and open archways lead to other rooms in the house. The mage guides us deep inside, entering the third open arch to our left.

"From what I know, him and my father never saw eye to eye. They were never close," Daren continues.

"That doesn't prove anything." Zoltan dismisses the explanation without missing a beat.

"Who never saw eye to eye?" Fenrir turns to look at us over the back of the leather couch he is sitting on.

"We have a problem." Zoltan is not taking chances with me, snatching me by the arm and plopping me on a two-seater before squeezing in next to me.

"Well, that's something new. Whatever will we do with an actual problem since we're not used to dealing with those at all?" Astara chirps, walking through the same entrance we used and carrying a tray with cups along with a steaming pot of what smells like tea. I wrinkle my nose and she laughs. "There is coffee and juice, too. His kitchen is well stocked for someone that doesn't leave Sienna often."

"I never said I don't leave Sienna often." Daren looks like he doesn't care that all the males in the room are staring daggers at him. "You assumed, but it seems to me that the time for secrets is long past. We are here and the wards and protections of this place will not let anyone get near without at least alerting me of another presence. Let's hear what all of us have to say."

"I'll feel better if Fenrir does his fancy juju too." When the Fae arches an eyebrow at my comment, I shoo away his arrogance with a closed fist. "I can't pronounce the illusion thing, so I'll just embarrass myself and butcher the shit out of it. Ward us off, please."

Fenrir tilts his head, reminding me how not human the Fae is, but the fact that he doesn't take his eyes off my fist almost makes me laugh. His eyes widen slightly, flicking from their usual blue to real black with white pupils, but it happens so fast I'm pretty sure I imagine it. When he finally looks at me, there is something akin to wonder all over his face. He gives me a slow nod.

"As you wish, fuil drágon." A soft breeze passes across my face as soon as he is done speaking. "We can talk freely."

I sit back because I'm tired to my bones, listening while the others bring Daren up to speed on everything that has happened since I entered the academy on my bike until he showed up through the portal. Absentmindedly, my thumb brushes over the stone of the necklace and I catch Fenrir flicking his gaze to it more than once. I wonder if the Fae can sense its presence or not, but that thought is squashed when Zoltan squeezes my thigh. It's official. I can't think when he is touching me. My whole body tunes in to his nearness and everything else fades to the background. Even when the mage spits out curses after hearing about the book and the Titans, it's still just a buzz in my ears.

"Yes, I am aware she is." Daren's voice snaps me out of my hormonal daze.

"What?" Looking from him to the others, I squeeze the stone hard enough for it to dig into my palm.

"I knew you are a dragon blood," Daren tells me like it's normal for him to know things about me that I had no clue about.

"How?" Pushing the words through clenched teeth, I force my fingers to lessen the pressure on the necklace.

"Your father, of course." Daren frowns at me. "You knew he used to come to my pub often."

"Not to discuss me I didn't." I'm not sure what angers me more, that he was talking to my father about me or that my father felt comfortable telling Daren what he never told me.

"He was worried about you, Franky." The mage shifts on his chair like he is uncomfortable. Well good, that makes two of us. "He asked me to keep an eye on you should something happen to him. I think he knew he was going to die."

Bile rises in the back of my throat. Zoltan gives me a comforting squeeze, but I slap his hand off my thigh. "That's why you befriended me? So I could let you close enough to keep an eye on me?"

"Wait a second, Franky." Daren leans forward beseechingly, but I see the guilty look crossing his eyes.

"Don't you Franky me, you liar. Answer the fucking question." I push each word through my teeth. "Is. That. Why. We. Became. Friends?" I don't dare to look at the others. I don't think I can handle if it I see pity in their eyes.

"I started talking to you because he asked me to. We ARE friends because of you and who you are." The mage looks insulted, but betrayal is still burning a hole in my chest.

"It doesn't matter now, does it?" I'll have a pity party

later when I'm alone. There are more important things to worry about. "What I want to know is who has Roberti been dealing with and is all of this somehow connected to my father's death? People come and go in your pub; you must've heard something."

"Apart from his typical informants, no one else as far as I was aware." Rubbing at his chin, he stares at the ground. "There were times when him and Aiden would take off up the hill, but whenever I heard anything to indicate he was dealing with the Daywalkers, it didn't raise any red flags at the time."

"Aiden." Spitting my ex partner's name like a curse, I want to slap myself for not thinking of it sooner. "That weasel will know something." A humorless laughter bursts out of me. "Of course, he will."

"He is the least of our concerns." Leo cracks his knuckles. "I'll pay him a visit as soon as we get back. He'll sing like a bird if he knows anything."

"You are certain that your uncle is dead?" Zoltan doesn't get sidetracked. The Daywalker is still dwelling on the gateway opening. "And you are the only other mage that can open a portal?"

"From what I know, yes." Daren squints at Zoltan. "I have no reason to lie to you Daywalker. I want to protect Sienna as much as you do."

"Sienna is the least of my worries." I jerk back from Zoltan and his words. He turns that penetrating gaze my way, nailing me in place. "Hear me now Francesca, and let them hear it too. If one hair is displaced from your head, the realms will be too small of a place for any of them."

The air entering my lungs is filled with some sort of expectancy. The rest of the people fade away and I sink into his too-blue gaze, which is promising things Zoltan has no right to offer. Tears prickle the corners of my eyes, but I force myself to blink them away because I will never let him see what those words mean to me. At least the dream they paint because the reality is very different. Not even the stubborn vampire can change the course of nature or the way our world functions, no matter how much both of us wish he could.

"How romantic," Astara gushes with her hands folded at her chest, breaking the snare I was in.

"Before we see what Aiden knows we might as well get my mother back." Pulling the leather satchel closer, I pet it fondly while changing the subject. "My daggers haven't seen action in a while, and I'd like to take them for a ride."

"That can be arranged." Daren jumps to his feet. "It's been a while since I have seen action too. It's time to brush off the rust."

"Just don't get yourself killed." When he smiles at me fondly, a sharp pang stabs me between the ribs. "We need the portals, but don't think I care too much about what happens to you after your treachery."

Daren grabs his chest dramatically as if I just stabbed him in the heart. Astara snickers and I can't stop myself from smiling for a split second. Lifting my hand to rub my forehead, the necklace slips through my fingers, the stone dangling in the air in front of my face. There is a collective sharp intake of breath.

"Serpentine," Fenrir says so reverently a shiver like a premonition crawls up my back.

Hopefully it's not a bad omen.

Chapter Thirteen

"We need to talk, Francesca." My hand pauses mid reach when Zoltan's voice drifts to me from the door in the kitchen.

"No sense of personal space and no care when someone asks for privacy when they need to think about things on their own." I snatch the glass out of the kitchen cabinet, slapping it closed. "You are quite the catch. I have no idea how any female resisted you until now."

"Avoiding me will not solve anything." Stubbornly, he leans his shoulder on the arched entrance, his arms folded like a shield in front of him. "What is it that spooked you so much? It's not the hunters for sure." There is a playful smirk on his lips, but his gaze is burning a hole in me.

"I'm not spooked," I lie shamelessly, avoiding looking straight at him. "We don't have time to worry about trivial things when everything is up in the air. Yes, we stopped Roberti from getting his greedy hands on the book, but I doubt that will stop him from bringing the Titans out.

When that happens, the hunters will be the least of our worries."

"How do you do it?" The genuine curiosity in his deep voice snaps my gaze to his face. "This"—He waves a hand encompassing my person— "pushing your personal life aside while going head-first into danger just to pretend it doesn't exist."

Sticky orange juice slushes over my hand when I overfill the glass, but I'm too stunned to notice because of the accuracy of his observation. Spitting obscenities under my breath, I grab a towel to blot it off of the counter. My body stiffens when he comes behind me, his hand closing over mine and stopping my frantic swiping.

"I don't want you to run from me." Zoltan presses closer, murmuring the words in my hair when he nuzzles me. "I won't let you." My knees wobble when he nips my ear.

"You think everything is about you." Steeling my spine, I stomp on the stupid butterflies fluttering in my stomach until all of them are turned into a pulp. *It's for the best*, I tell myself. "It never occurred to you that all I wanted was to scratch an itch and move on."

Something inside me dies when he turns into granite behind me.

"Scratch an itch?" Pulling away, his words come out so slow that each letter is like a dagger sinking in my heart. "That's what this is?"

"Was." My voice is calm and steady, unlike the screaming inside my head. "What this *was*, Zoltan."

Curling his fingers under my chin, he forcefully turns me to face him, holding my face so that I have no choice but to look him in the eye. I expect him to crush my jaw at any moment the way those digits are flexing. Determined to do the best performance of my life, I keep my eyes steady on his. Inside, though, every breath I take is killing me a little more.

"I am not a quick fuck to you." His gaze flicks on mine, searching, probing.

"You are one of the hottest males I have seen in my life. Why is it so strange to you that I would want to jump your bones?" *Please just leave so I can die in peace*, my mind screams desperately.

"You are a liar, Francesca." He flicks my face to the side, taking a step back. "If this is what you want, who am I to deny you?"

Sliding to the side on the kitchen counter, I don't turn to look at him again because I'm too afraid I'll start crying and apologizing for saying those words. My body is already missing the feeling of him being close to me. He stands there, the weight of his gaze like a noose around my neck, but I turn to the tall windows and stare unseeing at the forest beyond the clearing. It's early night in the human realm, not dark yet not light enough to see past the first row of trees in the distance.

"What time will we be leaving in search of my mother?" My voice sounds like a strangers to my own ears. Who is this person that sounds so collected and unfazed by ripping her own heart out? When he doesn't answer, I glance at him over my shoulder.

"As soon as Fenrir returns with the whereabouts of Roberti." A line forms between his eyebrows, and the vulnerable hesitation on his face is the last straw that extinguishes the spark of my soul.

I can see his mind working, going over everything that happened between us just like mine is. When uncertainty pulls those blue eyes to mine, I want to drop on my knees and beg him to forgive me for being stupid and cruel, but I stand in the same place, frozen, watching him war with himself. Coming to some decision that I'll never be privy of, he nods slowly at me.

"I never meant to presume, Ms. Drake. I apologize." Squaring his shoulders, he turns on his heel and walks out with his head held high, leaving me drifting in front of the window.

A slow clap makes me jump out of my skin.

"How very noble." Daren keeps clapping as he watches me with an unreadable expression. "And very stupid of you, Franky."

"This is none of your business, Daren." Taking a step forward, I sway on my feet, dizziness making the kitchen spin wildly.

"Easy there." The mage is right next to me, wrapping an arm around my waist. "For God's sake, you are as pale as a ghost."

"I'm fine, just a little lightheaded," I mumble under my breath, my lips numb and tingly.

Daren spits curses under his breath and ushers me to one of the chairs around a long wooden table at one end of the large kitchen. I let him do whatever he wants, too focused on how empty and hollow my chest feels. It's almost like my magic has shrunk away and wants nothing to do with me now. There is no heartbeat either. Shouldn't my heart keep pumping even if it's emotionally shredded to pieces. I'm sure that was true. Daren is living proof. The mage has a heartbeat. I'm sure of it because I can hear it even now.

Somewhere in the back of my mind I'm aware this is not a normal behavior, but I can't stop thinking insane thoughts or obsessing about why I can't hear my heart. My arms hang limply to my sides, sliding off my lap when Daren folds them there. Through a fog, I hear the mage yelling and calling for Astara. I'd like to tell him it's not a smart thing to do after I just insulted and hurt her brother, but my tongue is too thick in my mouth and I can't utter a word. Panic finally penetrates the cotton filling my head.

Leo and Astara come running inside the kitchen. I watch with wide eyes when Astara yanks on my shirt, pulling the necklace out. I forgot I put it over my head when Fenrir couldn't stop looking at it. Since I wasn't sure what the deal was, I hid it under my shirt. Leo is slapping my face and his lips are moving, but I can't hear a word. Scary, all-encompassing silence fills me, taking all that's Francesca Drake away from my physical body. Astara tugs on the chain sharply, breaking it. It dangles in her white-knuckled fist like a pendulum in my face.

All sound returns with a whoosh.

Sucking in a lungful of air, I cling to Leo's arms with trembling hands. Tears finally trickle over my cheeks in rivulets, soaking my shirt. All of them are talking but I can't answer from the crippling pain shredding my insides. A crazy thought crosses my mind. I can snatch the stone. It will stop me from feeling like this.

I dig my nails deeper into the alpha's skin.

"Drake." Leo shakes me to get my attention. "Francesca, what happened?"

"I knew it had something to do with this," Astara spits, looking at the stone in disgust.

"I've … had…" With my heart drumming in my throat, I can't speak until I've gulped many times to dislodge it. "I've had it around my neck since my father gave it to me. Nothing like this happened."

"Soren didn't awaken your dragon blood until you

entered the gates of the academy, right?" Daren is eyeing the stone warily. "I would bet my life it has something to do with that. Fenrir would know."

"You are not touching this until he comes back." Astara throws the necklace on the kitchen counter where it slides, finally stopping in the middle of it. "From the day I met you, I started thinking I'd have a short lifespan. Now I see why. You'll be the death of me, Franky."

"It's not like I did it on purpose." Grumbling, I can't stop my eyes from going to the arch entrance, but Zoltan is nowhere to be found. There is no way he missed all the shouting.

"He will come back." My head snaps at Daren when he speaks softly. "You are a good actress, I'll give you that, but blood never lies Franky. He has taken yours, so it's only a matter of time until he understands what you were doing."

"What did you do?" Astara narrows her eyes on me.

"What was right." I sound defensive but I can't help it. "What's taking Fenrir so long?"

"There were twenty-three different addresses for the Red Cross in the area where they held Zoltan." Leo pulls a chair out, flipping it around and straddling it. "It takes time to check them all out."

After I told them what Alexius was bragging about at the gala, we all decided that checking out the Red Cross was our best option. Alex is as arrogant as Roberti and I doubt it'll cross his mind that his words stuck with me. He made a very valid point at the time, though, which was his downfall. In this war, there is no place higher up the chain than being the one dealing with blood. You control the blood, then you control everything else. The question is: will they be dumb enough to hide in plain sight. Knowing Roberti as well as I do, I'd say yes. The asshole will gloat about being right under our noses. Now I just need Fenrir to return and confirm my suspicion.

And take Astara's glare away from me.

"What did you do?" Nobody could ever mistake her for anyone other than Zoltan's sister. Even if they didn't look alike, both are as stubborn as mules, not that I'm the one to talk.

"I set him free." My chin kicks up in defiance.

"You set him free." She deadpans, her chin hitting her chest.

"Yes, I did." Swallowing the tears that threaten to spill out, I wring my fingers under the table where she can't see them. "He is a pure blood and he will eventually find his mate, Astara. I'm grateful that all of you are so accepting and never make me feel like I'm less than you, but the fact of the matter is I'm a half blood. I can't be anyone's mate, least of all Zoltan's. He needs to move on instead of wasting his time on me."

"How noble of you." Her words are so condescending they're dripping like honey from her voice.

"That's what I said." Daren snickers, but chokes on it when I scowl at him.

"Can we not talk about this, please?" Shifting uncomfortably on the chair, I roll my neck to relieve the tension building at the back of my skull. "There are more concerning matters."

"Oh, we are talking about this alright." Jamming both fists on her hips, Astara looks down her nose at me like some teacher. "You two, get out," she barks at Leo and Daren.

If I expect backup or even them telling her off for daring to kick them out, I'm sorely disappointed. Both males jump up like someone poured scolding hot water over their heads and scurry out of the kitchen like cockroaches. I'm left gaping at the empty doorway with my heart hammering like a frightened bird in my chest.

"Let me hear what other bullshit is going through your head, Franky." She twirls her hand in my face, wordlessly telling me not to try her patience.

"It's not bullshit if it's true." Indignation makes me straighten in my chair. "It's what the fates have in store for us, no matter if we like it or not."

"And you became an expert on fate and destiny when?"

"Don't patronize me, not you please." Leaning my elbows on the table, I grab fistfuls of my hair. "The longer I let it go on, the harder it'll be on me when it ends. Maybe it's selfish but I can't take it. Not with him." When I look at her again, I'm taken aback by her teary-eyed expression instead of the pissed-off one from a second ago.

"Do you know why he and Fenrir are so adamant about you not taking the oath?" Pushing a chair close to mine, she sits down next to me and takes my hands in hers.

I shake my head mutely.

"You have to make a sacrifice for the oath to be binding." She squeezes my fingers. "You need to give up something that means everything to you for it to count. The magic they use will take nothing else. Everything has a price."

I can't swallow the lump forming like a fist in my throat.

"Do you know what my brother sacrificed for that oath?" My mouth opens but no words come out, and Astara's face blurs through the tears gathering in my lashes. A fat tear rolls out and trickles down, clinging to my chin for a long moment before disappearing when it splatters over our joined hands. "He gave up his right to a true mate. For what it's worth, his destiny is the same as yours. At least in this."

Squeezing my eyes shut doesn't lessen the stabbing pain in my chest.

"A blind person can see how much he means to you, Franky." More tears roll from my closed eyes while she speaks. "He knows that too. Unless he is dumb. Males can be dumb about things like this."

I bark out a laugh and she chuckles.

"He needs a moment to realize what you were doing, I'm sure." Standing up, she pulls me to my feet. "Don't push him away a second time. Okay?" At my nod, she throws her arms around me. "Your heart was in the right place, but you are so stupid for willingly giving up something good, fates be damned."

"I feel lost in this new world that Soren pushed me in." It's easier to talk when my face is hidden in her hair. "I don't know what is up and what is down anymore." A door crashes open and we jerk away from each other. Fenrir storms in like a hurricane inside the foyer, his voice bouncing around the entire house.

"I found them!"

Chapter Fourteen

Absentmindedly rubbing the center of my chest, I try, and miserably fail, to pay attention to what Fenrir is saying. I hear the words, but I don't understand a thing. It's like he is speaking some foreign language. Bits and pieces filter through about taking a left turn on some street in Santa Monica, then some industrial park with shipping containers until I zone out again. The remnants of the numb, empty feeling inside me lingers, sinking its claws between my ribs and clinging there so I can't get rid of it.

"Drake, you paying attention here or do we bore you?" Blinking stupidly at Leo, I realize he is talking to me.

"Sorry, what?" With a frustrated grunt, the Alpha throws his hands in the air. "I'm listening, we need to go to Santa Monica to a shipping center."

Astara chortles.

"Is that all you heard?" Pinching his nose between a thumb and forefinger, Fenrir has his eyes closed as if in pain.

"Yes?" Uncertainty laces my question as my eyes snap to each of their faces.

"What is going on with you?" The Fae frowns at me like I'm a child having a tantrum.

"Nothing is going on with me." Anger spikes up, but it's aimed at me, not at Fenrir, though my words still come out sharp. "Why do we have to sit and debate everything with you guys? You found the assholes, now let's go kill them. A long conversation isn't needed. We need action."

You can hear a pin drop.

"If you were listening as you should've been"—Staring down his nose at me, which is his usual way, Fenrir clenches his fists. "You know they'll have the entire building warded. The place is locked down tight, and they will shred anyone without clearance to walk through."

"I thought it was a blood bank thingy." Dropping my hand under the table, I poke at the seam of my pants with a nail. "Don't they need humans walking in and out all the time? How does that work?"

"That's what we are trying to figure out," Astara says while glaring at Leo and Fenrir.

With a sigh, I slump in the chair. "I'm sorry. I'm still a little rattled from earlier." When Astara's head turns to me with a snap, I grind my teeth. "About the stone," I clarify in case she decides to talk about her brother and the cluster-fuck I created.

Speaking of which, the Daywalker is still nowhere to be found. Out of desperation I tried opening the link between us only to find an impenetrable wall blocking any attempt to feel him. It's what I wanted a couple of hours ago, but now it's like a dagger stuck in my chest. One I can't remove no matter how hard I try. I've done many stupid things in my life, but this one tops the scale by a long shot.

"What happened with the stone?" Fenrir's gaze is so intent on me my skin prickles in awareness.

"I couldn't breathe and started feeling empty." Rolling my shoulders to get rid of the phantom sensation, I stare at the Fae's chin because I'm unable to meet his eyes. "It numbed me ... I think ..." trailing off, I flick a quick glance at those penetrating eyes but regret it the same second.

"Her skin was very pale, almost silverish in hue." Squinting at me in thought, Astara's words are slow and measured. "Her hair was changing too, whiter than anything I've seen. Almost like frost was taking over the strands." She turns to the Fae and her mouth forms a thin line. "You know anything about it?"

"It's over now." Fenrir is still staring at me without saying a word, and it makes me want to squirm. "It's off."

"Where is it?" I jump at his barked question.

Pretending I don't notice my shaky finger, I point at the kitchen counter where Astara threw the stupid thing. What scares me more than what that stone can do to me is the uncontrolled power coming from Fenrir, blasting all of us like a furnace. Astara has already moved, now partially standing in front of me in a protective stance. Daren is stiff as a board and Leo has his upper lip curled in a half snarl. It's affecting all of us, but the Fae is oblivious, rushing to the counter like his life depends on it. With a sigh of relief, he snatches the broken necklace in his hand, all the strain and uncontrolled pulses draining out of him the same instant.

Wariness slithers up my spine like a venomous snake.

"What's that stone, Fenrir?" Each word coming out of my mouth is slow and cautious.

"Serpentine." Again, the reverence in his voice makes my heart pound like a fist against my breastbone.

"I've never heard of it." I turn to Daren when he

speaks, seeing his face scrunched up with his eyebrows lowered like he is trying to remember something with no luck.

"You wouldn't, mage. Stay away from it." I'm taken aback when Fenrir rounds on him with a sneer.

"Yo!" My shout jerks his head my way. "As far as I can see, none of us have heard of it. Only you have. You don't have to be an asshole about it."

"I apologize." Drawing in a deep breath that puffs up his chest enough to stretch his t-shirt within an inch of its life, Fenrir blows it out and calms himself down. He doesn't look at Daren, though he is looking at me so I scowl at him.

"To him." Hitching a thumb at the mage, I dare the Fae to argue. "Not to me."

"I apologize." Pushing the words through clenched teeth, Fenrir looks pained that he has to do it.

"What is it?" The Fae looks startled that I'm asking him this question. "Is it a weapon? Like a kryptonite for dragon blood or something? Cause sure as fuck didn't try to kill me when I was a pesky half blood."

"Kryptonite?" Leo whispers, turning his head between Astara and Daren as if looking for help.

"Yeah, you know, like that rock that almost killed Superman?" The alpha looks more confused than ever, so I dismiss him with a wave of my hand. "Never mind, all of you live under a rock. No surprise the hunters have been multiplying. You still live in the Middle Ages or something."

"Who is Superman?" Leo mumbles, at Daren but the mage shakes his head to shut him up.

"Well?" Ignoring the poor shifter that is now looking dismayed and a little freaked out, I lock my gaze on the Fae. "What is it, or more importantly what can it do?"

"I would rather have this conversation between us Francesca." Fenrir's chin kicks up stubbornly.

"Too fucking bad for you, Fae." Twirling a finger to encompass everyone, I grin at him humorously. "See this bunch? You and I are stuck with them, and if it wasn't for their fast reactions, I would've been a corpse you found when you got back. So, speak up. The cat is out of the bag, so you might as well add more to it since they haven't started running … yet."

"Remember what you said to me when I asked what court you were from?" My breath freezes in my lungs at Zoltan's voice.

The vampire is leaning one shoulder on the arched entrance, his arms folded over his massive chest. He changed clothing, wearing dark jeans that wrap around his powerful thighs like they are giving him a hug. A faded dark blue t-shirt with some writing on it is stretched over his pectorals, the words too washed out to be readable. The sleeves are tight, digging into his biceps where his muscles twitch under my scrutiny. Droplets soak up the fabric on his shoulders, dripping from his still-wet hair. My gaze sweeps over him, stopping at his bare feet, his legs crossed at the ankle in a relaxed manner. I would've believed the nonchalance if it wasn't for his eyes.

Those blue peepers burn with some emotion that I can't decipher, and it turns my heartbeat into an erratic fluttering in my chest. It would've been wonderful if I could say the sensation is lust. But, no. What blooms inside me when we lock gazes is fear like I've never felt around any Daywalker before. The too-blue gaze is burning, but it's empty and calculating at the same time. And I can't feel shit from him through the blood connection. I'm still hitting that damn wall he placed between us. *Way to go, Franky, you idiot.*

I gulp thickly.

"I'm one of the Courtless Fae." I croak out, and there is a collective intake of breath. Fenrir staring daggers at Zoltan.

Zoltan looks at Fenrir with no change in his expression.

"Serpentine is a stone only found in Faery. In our realm." A muscle is jumping in Fenrir's jaw and his hands are in white-knuckled fists. "Even there, it's a closely-guarded stone and a well-kept secret among the Fae protecting it."

"Okay." I drag out the word, but uneasiness is already shriveling my lungs.

"The Courtless Fae, to be more specific." The Fae turns his furious gaze on me, and my blood curdles in my veins from that look.

"So, they ... I mean *we* are guardians of it?" A hysterical giggle bursts out of me. It's not that bad if it's a guardian thing. I can live with that. I'm a half blood and the stupid thing didn't like me. Big fucking deal. I hate the damn stone too, so we are even.

"Serpentine can be found only in one place, even for the Courtless Fae." All of a sudden Zoltan is a chatty Cathy when any other time you have to pry words out of his mouth.

"What, were you a Fae in your previous life or did they hire you as a PR?" I hiss at him then bite my tongue hard to shut myself up and stop talking.

The sound coming out from Daren is pained but I don't move my glare away from the infuriating male. I mean, what the fuck really? Can't they just come out with it and say whatever it is? I'm already pruning inside and soon enough I'll turn into a husk from the unknown. It's my ass on the line here, so I deserve to know if that damn stone can kill me. Or why it wants to kill me might be a better question. The permanent smirk tilts up Zoltan's lips but it's not the like before. It looks practiced, fake.

"The throne of the Courtless Fae is made of serpentine." Fenrir sounds like his life is leaving him with that sentence. "It's the only serpentine in all the realms."

My mouth opens then closes a few times.

"And now comes the question of how you ended up in a possession of it." Voice full of suspicion, Zoltan pushes off the wall.

"My father gave it to me, which I already said." Seeing him walk toward me, I lift off the chair, not wanting to have to crane my neck to look at him. "I didn't hide who gave it to me."

Astara steps between us but Zoltan throws her away with a shoulder, sending her body into Fenrir. I'm too shocked at the murderous look on the vampire's face to react or even think of defending myself. I never expected him to look at me this way, and at this moment I understand why everyone is afraid of him. I've seen him pissed but it has never been aimed at me, until now.

He strikes fast as a snake, his thick, strong fingers wrapping around my neck and lifting me off the ground. On reflex, my hands jerk to his wrist, my nails clawing and scratching his skin in hopes he will let go. With the air being cut off from my lungs, dark spots dance at the corners of my eyes, and my legs kick wildly, the tips of my boots scraping over the floor. My chest is burning for oxygen, but my head is already filled with cotton and I can't think. The others are shouting trying to get him to see reason but he uses his mind fuck powers muting them up. It never even occurs to me to fight him back. Not until the entity sharing my body perks up.

Fury like I've never known before blasts through me. How can anyone dare to think they can hurt me twice? The world is bathed in pulsing red lights. Flashes of a feral Zoltan draining my blood play on repeat, flickering like an old movie in front of me. It feels like I'm being reminded of what he almost did not long ago. The instinct to breathe disappears, leaving the knowledge that I don't need oxygen to live. It should freak me out, but Zoltan is still squeezing my neck like he wants to pop my head off and I can't think straight. My head tilts to the side, my vision expanding and retracting until it settles down, and the Daywalker's eyes widen in shock.

"Na dèan an Daywalker seo." Goosebumps cover me head to toe from the sound of my voice.

"Don't do this, Daywalker," Fenrir translates, his voice strained like he is the one being choked to death. He might be compelled to speak since he was under Zoltan's influence until now.

"Is urrainn dhomh do mharbhadh gun smaoineachadh." The hissing and sinuous quality of the foreign sounds coming out of my mouth chill my soul.

"I can kill you without thinking," Fenrir chirps this part a little too eagerly, and a grin stretches my lips. "She can in this state, just so you are aware."

With a harsh jerk, Zoltan drops me from his grasp and stumbles back, a horrified expression twisting his handsome face. A trickle of pain that he will be disgusted by me tries to push through, but I'm not in control of my body or my actions at the moment. Just a passenger in my skin suit going for the ride. I watch him calmly with my hands hanging limply at my sides while many expressions fleet through his features, until he clenches his jaw so hard I can hear his teeth grinding and scraping together.

"Math," I hiss at him, still smiling.

"Good," the Fae translates and gives Zoltan a wide berth, skirting around him to get closer to me.

"I know what math means." The vampire glares at Fenrir, and everyone sags when he releases the influence he had on them.

Fenrir jerks a shoulder up, unimpressed at Zoltan's hostility while giving me side-eyed glances. I can feel the prissy entity slowly retracting from my mind, shrinking back in my chest where it resides. The last thing to disappear is the light-bright colors in my vision and I almost miss them when they're gone. The world looks dull and washed out, everything lacking the vibrancy and life I see through the dragon eyes. Well, it looks dull until I lock gazes with Zoltan. Nothing can dull the too-intense color of his blue eyes.

"What the hell is the matter with you?" I rasp when pain slams me like a sledgehammer, my neck burning from the inside.

"How is it you have that stone?" There is still accusation in Zoltan's tone but his Adam's apple bobs as he swallows thickly.

"Why does it fucking matter you crazy asshole? You almost killed me!" I regret screaming because it shreds the inside of my throat more. It hurts like a bitch.

"Because no one has seen that stone in centuries." Zoltan roars in my face, forcing me to flinch. "And no one but the royals had access to that stone. Do you know what the royal Courtless Fae are? Heartless assassins, with no remorse who care about no one else apart from themselves. I understand now everything you said to be the truth."

I jerk back like he slaps me.

Well, fuck. Here I go again at the top of the to-be-killed-on-sight list.

"Yay!" I pump my fist in the air, but sadly no one joins my little celebration of insanity.

Chapter Fifteen

"Are you sure about this?" Fenrir asks for the fifth time, and all I can do is sigh.

"Yes, Fenrir. I'm sure." Rubbing little circles on my temples doesn't help at all with the splitting headache that gives me a second heartbeat pounding behind my eyes.

After our little drama in Daren's kitchen, Zoltan leaves to go who knows where and the rest of us stand in stunned silence. It lasts exactly two minutes before everyone starts talking at once, and when trying to tell them to stop shouting doesn't work, I promptly faint. Yes, I know, not one of my finest moments, but everything got to be too much and my brain just switched off. It was lights out. Then I wake up to everyone still arguing between each other.

I have no idea how I convinced them to head out and find my mother but here we are. Zoltan decided to join us but he kept as far away from me as possible. All of us crammed inside an SUV. Daren looked too smug pulling out from around his house with the vehicle, fretting around it like a mother hen. I expected him to start kissing the hood of the car. It was priceless to see his face when Tenebris decided to grace us with his presence after he had been missing.

The panther shoved Daren out of his way, jumping through the driver's door and scratching the shit out of the leather seats with his claws until he settled in the back seat. Right now, I'm squished against the window and the door is stabbing my hip and ribs on one side, while Fenrir jabs his elbow in my arm on the other. Astara and Leo are in the same situation on the other side of Tenebris, all because the feline refused to move from the center of the seat. He sits perched straight like a freaking Egyptian statue of Bast as he stares through the windshield unblinking. He is not fazed by my glares either. Typical cat.

"We can't be sure that you can go through the wards." Astara sounds irritated but I know it's not at me. The alpha is the reason for her agitation.

I hide my grin.

"We can try." I'm willing to try anything just so I don't have to deal with the rest of the shitstorm my life is turning out to be. Shredded by deadly wards? Count me in. "Worst case scenario, I die. It's a win, win," I add it a little too cheerfully.

Zoltan stiffens in the passenger seat.

When the vampire's shoulders bunch up so he can turn around to look at me, the panther makes a horrible sound in his throat, which changes his mind. My arms pebble and I give Tenebris a quick glance, but he is staring daggers at the back of Zoltan's head. He can't know what happened between Zoltan and me because he wasn't there. Or so I think anyway. Maybe he enjoyed the show too much to intervene. No one can say that cats are not assholes no matter the size.

"We will find a way in, Franky." Daren puts as much confidence in his words as he can while clutching the steering wheel like he wants to strangle it. I bet he is imagining it's Tenebris's neck. "If we can't, I'll make us one."

"Did you happen to see how many of them are in the place?" Zoltan turns his face addressing the Fae.

My stomach clenches tight when the lights we are passing play on his high cheekbones and full lips. His thick, long lashes create shadows on his skin and no matter how upset I am with him for his behavior, I must admit only to myself that he is absolutely breathtaking. *And you told him you just used him for a quick fuck you dumbass.* I bite the inside of my mouth hard when my inner voice decides to be a jerk.

"I saw a handful on the outside parameter, but I can't be sure how many are inside." Fenrir shifts next to me, jabbing me again with his elbow. "I'm certain they are guarding someone because they were strategically placed. Two at the front, three on the roof, and three at the back. Even if I missed one or two that could've been walking around at the time, that's still a number we can deal with."

With a grunt of affirmation, Zoltan turns away, making me miss his stupidly handsome face. I groan at my own idiocy, shaking my head when Fenrir looks at me with a raised eyebrow. You can't get more pathetic than this. A male tries to drain you dry and you have sex with him. Then he tries to strangle the shit out of you but your heart speeds up just looking at him. Maybe one of these days I will realize I have a serious problem. Stockholm syndrome I think the humans call it. That's it.

"What about Stockholm syndrome?" Astara leans forward to look at me around Tenebris, her eyebrows lifted all the way to her hairline.

Damn it, I must've spoken out loud.

"Nothing." Murmuring under my breath with my cheeks burning in embarrassment, I turn to stare out the window.

"Left here." Fenrir leans forward, eagerly saving me from further questions. "We can leave the car a block down and go the rest of the way on foot. It's open space around the place, they'll see us if we drive further than that."

Gnawing on my mouth, I hold my breath just like the rest of them. With all the pent-up energy I've been pushing to the back of my mind just so I don't have to deal with it, I pray to anyone who will listen that Roberti is here. I'd love to take my anger out on him. Or Alex. I'll take that asshole as a second-best option, too.

Daren glides the cumbersome vehicle to the side of the road behind an abandoned van with graffiti covering it and bricks instead of wheels. We all pile out as fast as we can, stretching out the kinks in our muscles from being lined up like sardines inside. The last to come out is Tenebris, gracefully jumping from the back seat as fresh as a daisy. Frowning, I watch him stretch, arching his back this way and that without a care in the world. What's his deal anyway?

"Is there a reason the cat is tagging along?" I aim the question at Fenrir under my breath, but Tenebris pauses in his twisting, one of his ears twitching my way.

"With all that's been happening, I forgot to say anything about it." Rubbing the back of his neck, Fenrir looks flustered. My eyebrow crawls up my forehead and he gives me a sheepish look. "Ever since he gave his oath, he has been in his shifted form. What Argoz was shocked about was the fact that Tenebris never comes close to the academy. We all knew he was somewhere in the forest around it, but no one has seen him in a very long time." His eyes flick to the panther, who is paying close attention to our hushed conversation while pretending otherwise. "Until now."

"Another first. Go me!" I grumble but cut off everything else I am about to say when Tenebris snaps his head my way.

"I don't think you understand, Hellion." The Fae gives the panther an apologetic look. "I don't think he was aware that he would be sacrificing his human form when he was asked to give the oath. Even the Board had guards posted around them who were tight for years after that. The fact that he came now ... for you ..."

He doesn't have to say the rest. I'm well aware how all this will look to the old jerks sitting up on their highchairs. Not that I need another reason for them to hate me, but why the hell not. Just one more thing going against me.

Tenebris is still watching me with his jewel-colored eyes unblinking, and I can't help but wonder what is going through his head. Does he see me as something that is at the academy to stir the pot, something that is nothing more than entertainment for the Board, or is it more than that? The fact that he was in that forest when I first went through it doesn't surprise me at all. A lot of things are lurking between those trees. Things I never want to come across. But that means Soren knew. And if that ancient Fae was aware, I have a bad feeling that he had something to do with all of this.

"Let's go, we've lingered enough." Daren breaks through my musings and I finally look away from the panther.

Following close at the mage's heels, I ignore the fact that Zoltan is walking as far away from me as possible. Convincing myself that it doesn't bother me and that his hoovering is only one thing pissing me off about him, I keep my gaze straight, focusing on where we are going. The neighborhood looks mostly abandoned. Industrial buildings line both sides of the street, their chained fences locked with heavy padlocks, trash sprinkled around the front yards, and the windows boarded with nailed-on plywood. Vandals have had the time of their lives painting over the walls or ripping the plywood off and leaving it hanging askew at random. The salty tinge in the air is teasing my nostrils, mixing with the stench of urine and making me wrinkle my nose.

It's impossible to miss the place we are going. The Fae said it had wards to keep everyone away. What he forgot to mention is the tall walls like some damn high security prison with barbed wire stretched between metal poles all around it. Scratch that, not metal poles. Silver poles. I give him a glare but Fenrir just shrugs, grinning at me like a fool. And they keep saying I'm the one with a death wish. On top of that, we stayed at Daren's house longer than necessary so the night is almost gone, the sky already lightening from pitch black to some stupid shade of gray that is laughing in my face at the fact that I'll go blind here if I don't get out of dodge by the time the sun comes up. The stakes just went up a notch for Franky.

Another typical day in the life of Francesca Drake in other words.

Daren lifts a hand, stopping our silent progression. Turning to face us since we followed behind him, he points left and right of the building, showing us two fingers in each direction. It's good that we are splitting up. Eagerness stirs in the pit of my stomach, and when Leo and Astara peel off to the right, Fenrir tugs on my arm and pulls me along with him to the left. So, no Zoltan, see if I care. Tenebris slinks along my thigh, coming with me with his tail lashing the air.

I peer over my shoulder one last time to see Daren and

Zoltan move like wraiths towards the tall metal gates before we turn a corner around the high walls. The mage is already moving his hands in front of him, thick liquid like lava bubbling between them. Rushing to catch up with Fenrir, I swallow the unease I feel about this. I'm just used to the infuriating vampire breathing down my neck, that's all. I don't need him next to me to get this done.

We reach the middle of the wall, the bricks stretching long on both sides. The Fae stops craning his neck up and I follow suit. It's easily three stories high, and when I look back at his face a groan rumbles from my chest to see him smiling from ear to ear. Not rock climbing again. Playing Spiderman once was enough to last me a lifetime.

Fenrir jumps up, agile like a damn circus performer as he crawls on the wall with incredible speed. His ass tightens with each shift of his legs and I'd have to be blind not to look at it. Until he stops moving and my eyes snap to his face. The Fae winks at me, his white teeth blinking from his wide smile. Cursing up a storm—I might've invented a word or two in the process—I search for a place to grab so I can start climbing. I feel bad for Leo because if Astara breaks a nail she will no doubt blame it on him.

Deciding on a brick, my knees bend slightly to jump for it. I bite down the scream that lodges in my throat when the panther shoves his head in my ass and gives me a hard push. Scrambling up the wall, I keep telling myself that regardless of him being a shifter and having a higher intelligence than a panther would have, Tenebris, at the moment, is an animal. Well more animal than human in any case. There is nothing weird about having him stick his head between my legs. Nothing at all. He is just trying to help. It's a good thing this happened because I reach the top where Fenrir is waiting for me without realizing it. My arms and legs are burning so I don't complain much when the Fae grabs my arms and pulls me the rest of the way up like a rag doll.

We both crouch on the top of the wall, the barbed wire an inch from our faces. The panther crawls up last, slinking on his belly further away to give us enough space without pushing us over. The building on the other side of the wall looks too ordinary to be hosting the likes of Roberti or the hunters I can see pacing at the front and on the roof. Blades glint in what's left of the moonlight, which tells me they are armed to their teeth. This might not be as easy as we originally thought.

"Now what?" My question is barely above a whisper, but my heart stops when the five hunters I can see turn their faces our way.

No way they heard what I said.

Everything happens at once.

Bright reflector lights blind me, disorienting me. Fenrir shouts something, but a burst of electricity blasts us from the barbed wire and sends him flying off the wall. I can hear Tenebris roaring in outrage, but I can't see shit to save my life. And just when I think I'm about to follow the Fae off the wall and end up breaking my neck, thick energy wraps around me like a lasso, tugging me forward. My eyes scrunch expecting the wire to rip my face into ribbons, but I'm lifted in the air above its sharp, pointy spikes. My stomach drops at my feet and blinding pain from my skin catching on fire opens my mouth in a silent scream.

Everything goes black.

Chapter Sixteen

I come to with a gasp and a feeling that I would rather be dead.

If I got hit by a truck, stomped on by a stampede of angry bulls, and tossed around by a tornado, I bet I will feel better than I do right now. Tasting acid in my mouth makes me gag, but I neither have the energy to lift my head, nor to vomit. The burning of my shoulders tells me my arms are pulled back and my wrists tied. That's a stupid oversight for whoever did this because I've been in a similar situation too many times to count and I'm a pro at getting out of it, if I say so myself. That idea perks me up a little, just enough to feel like I might puke.

With great effort I lift my head, huffing and puffing to blow the hair out of my face so I can see where I am. A sterile white room is what I find. No windows, just white walls on all sides with a heavy metal door in front of me. It looks like a vault door from what I can see. My eyes move around, methodically searching each line and corner from floor to ceiling in search of cameras. Not finding anything, I take a deep breath.

The door opens with a hissing sound, as if it was sealed shut until now. My body stiffens and I'm grateful I didn't try to free myself too soon. Then I regret it the moment Alexius walks in with a twinkle of amusement in his peepers and a smile to match. The asshole is gloating.

I grin back at him.

"Fancy seeing you here, Alex." My cheerfulness is lost on the jerk but his smile slips. "Long time no see."

"How did I know that you'd come here, Francesca?" Stabbing his hands in the pockets of his slacks, he walks nonchalantly up and down in front of me. "Or should I call you, Franky?" Flashing me a quick smile, he shakes his head at some joke I missed.

"How about you don't call me anything?" Lifting both eyebrows, I keep the grin in place mocking him. "There's an idea for you."

"I didn't believe Roberti when he told us if we took your mother you'd come for her." Nodding his head, Alex decides to have a monologue so I let him. "Never pegged you as mama's girl."

I nod eagerly like an idiot when he looks at me, and that makes him frown.

"I must say I never expected Tenebris." Striding fast, he stops in front of me, snatching my chin between his fingers and jerking my face up. "This is why half-bloods need to be destroyed. You will bring the end of us all just by being allowed to exist." His blunt nails dig into my skin, squeezing so tight I expect my jaw to break any second.

Tears sting my eyes, but I force them back. Hopefully the entity inside me will stay quiet for a while longer. I have plans for this jerk and I want to be myself when I get my hands on him. No additional help needed.

"It's a good thing we got rid of him and Fenrir at the same time. The Fae always got on my nerves." My heart jerks hitting the roof of my mouth, and Alex smiles slowly, his mouth stretching until I can see his molars. "I hoped it'd be Zoltan." His head cocks to the side. "Problem in paradise already?"

"Nope." It's hard to speak with him holding my chin, but the fact he doesn't know Zoltan is here almost makes me laugh. "I just like to spice things up. Different flavor each day if you may. It keeps things fresh and interesting. You should try it." Faking a frown, I widen my eyes. "No wait, I'm sorry. How insensitive of me. You let Roberti fuck you every which way he wants so that's probably the only flavor you need."

I haven't finished talking when the back of his hand connects with my face in a loud smack. If my face wasn't messed up earlier, I bet my life it is now because I feel my cheekbone crack from the force of his hit. Blood fills my mouth when I bite hard on my tongue. That will teach me to run my mouth while being slapped around, won't it. Having Alexius being so open, though, is something I plan to take full advantage of.

"Smart of you to hold my mother here, I'll give you that." Wiping the corner of my mouth on my shoulder, I relish the sharp pain when my tied wrists shift. "But she is meek, so you didn't need to go through all the trouble." I have a lisp when I talk from nearly biting off my tongue.

"Meek?" There is no way he fakes that incredulity. I grin internally. "You must be talking about someone else." Anger laces his words.

"Umm, I know my mother. She is afraid of her own

shadow, unless you snatched the wrong person?" Tilting my head to the side, I give him a wary look. "I can't go to Sienna so I'm not sure it's her that you have here. Roberti would know, so, where is he?"

I am waiting for uncertainty to enter his gaze. On one side, it's good to have him doubt himself, but on the other, it means the jerk Roberti is not here. You can't win it all, I guess. Keeping the wariness plastered over my face, I let him mule it over. He better hurry because it won't be long before the others blast their way in. All my acting skills will go to waste if I'm still tied up here like a Christmas present.

"I was certain …" Alex trails off, giving me a sharp look.

Spinning on his heel, he rushes out of the room muttering under his breath. I sit still and call out his name a couple of times before I press my lips closed. *Don't lay it on too thick, Franky.* Telling myself that, I snicker quietly when the door sucks in air to seal itself shut. Opening it might be a problem, but Alexius will have to come back eventually. I'll be ready to give him the same facial he gave me when that happens.

I stiffen my shoulders before dislocating my thumb. It smarts to hell and back, but I bite my lips so I don't cry out. With a deep breath I fill my lungs, holding it in as I do the same to my other thumb. My arms are numb from pain all the way to my elbows, but I wiggle out of the ties holding me stuck to the chair. With a sigh of relief, I roll my shoulders to loosen my arms before pushing my thumbs in. My entire body hurts, and my cheekbone is throbbing, but I smile despite all that. I'll have to send a gift basket to a wild pack of wolves in Sienna when I get back. The little shits managed to tie me up quite a few times before I locked their asses up. Thanks to them, I'm free now and ready for Alex to return if I can't open the door.

I don't have to wait long. I've barely stood next to it with my back plastered to the wall for five minutes when the now familiar hiss alerts me someone is coming in. Bracing to fight my way out of here the second a head peeks in, I grab whoever it is by the neck, twisting my body and yanking them inside and over my shoulder. The air is pushed out of his lungs with a whoosh and I flip around, jumping on his chest with my arm cocked to pulverize his face. I have a second to see Leo's wide, startled eyes moving my hand slightly to the right and smashing it into the floor with a resounding crunch. There go my fucking knuckles. They just joined my fractured cheekbone. My eyes cross from the pain and a buzzing starts in my ears.

"Damn it, Drake, you'll give a male a heart attack." Growling, he bucks me off him while I'm still seeing stars.

"I almost gave you a new face, dumbass, so stop bitching and say thank you." Voice strained, I roll to my feet while cradling my hand to my chest. "Fenrir? Tenebris?" I hold my breath, watching Leo's face intently to see if he is telling the truth.

"Dazed and sore, but good." Rushing to the door, he pokes his head out before pulling it almost closed. "That is some strong shit they are packing on those walls. Lucky Daren was already messing with the wards, otherwise both of them would be gone."

"They are alive." I breathe the words while swaying on my feet. I wasn't aware how much I was freaking out inside thinking they were dead.

"Their pride is hurt but they are alive." Throwing a quick smirk, he sobers up instantly. "Tenebris is fucking furious, killing everything that crosses his path. I'm not sure he can tell a friend from a foe so stay out of his way."

"Like he wasn't an asshole before this happened." I'm so happy they are okay that I'll let the stupid cat bite my hand off just to see him alive with my own eyes.

"You ready?" Leo leans in closer to the door listening for something. I can't hear a thing over the pounding in my ears. "We need to go before all hell breaks loose."

A loud crash like half of the building is collapsing comes right when he stops speaking. A scream follows. "Too late for that." I debate only a second before yanking Leo deeper into the room and closing the door.

"Are you insane?" Snarling at me, he jerks his arm out of my grasp.

"Alex was here not long ago." I twirl a finger around my throbbing cheekbone. "This is the first place he will run to."

"Or he will wait wherever he has your mother for you to go to him." He grumbles but follows suit, flattening himself on the other side of the door.

"Or that."

Changing my mind, I run back to the chair, plopping on it and hitting my tailbone in the process. Pulling my arms back like they are still tied, I shake my head to mess up my hair around my face. The alpha is watching me with morbid curiosity, and I chuckle when he opens and closes his mouth with a snap. Leo stiffens a second before the door opens and Alexius storms in.

I blink at him innocently.

"You fucking bitch." Rage twisting his features, he rushes me.

Leo doesn't have time to push away from the wall. Alex is in front of me so fast I almost receive another blow to the head for being surprised by it. Ducking my head, I push hard off the chair, my shoulder hitting his solar plexus as I tackle him to the ground. He is so shocked that I'm free that I have time to roll us around and straddle his chest, trapping both his arms between my thighs. I allow myself one grin at his stupefied expression before pummeling his face with my fists. The knuckles on my right hand make me see stars from hitting the floor earlier but the satisfaction of cracking Alexius's skull is much stronger.

With a roar, he jerks his arms wide to the side then up, pitching me forward over his head. I am so focused on hitting him I forget to make sure he is well pinned under me. Tucking my head to my chest at the last second, I barely avoid face planting on the floor, rolling away from him and ending up in a crouch a couple of feet away. Face bloodied and nose flattened, Alex snarls at me, his fangs sticking out from his split lips. There is a piece of his upper lip hanging by skin on the right side of his face, exposing the top of his gums. I've never seen a more beautiful sight. His entire body should look like that. Behind him, Leo is gaping at us frozen in place.

"I've been called worse," I tell Alexius before pouncing on him again.

We meet halfway, both of us jumping at each other at the same time. He flings his elbow in front of him just as I reach him, connecting with my neck. I can feel my esophagus flattening but it still works, so I blink away the tears and turn my head to the rip into Alexius's throat. My fangs sink in deep and I shake like a feral dog, pulling chunks of his muscle with me. Blood gushes from the mauled nick but he is too far gone to notice. His own fangs get stuck in my shoulder, almost taking a chunk of my collarbone when he pulls back. Seeing his wounds close as soon as he takes my blood send a sharp zing of panic through me.

"Oh no you don't." With a furious snarl, I take his head in my hands and twist around with everything I got.

My shoulder takes the brunt of my fall, and I roll for a few feet, taking Alexius with me as I clutch his head for dear life. As soon as I stop, I'm on my knees, fangs bared to rip into him all over again. Blinking stupidly, I look at Alex's wide eyes. His unseeing eyes because I'm clutching his head in my hands without the body that goes with it. Very slowly, I uncramp my fingers and release it on the floor with a wet squelchy sound. Wiping my hands off my blood-soaked pants, I pull my gaze away from the head to lock on Leo.

"Remind me to never piss you off again, Drake." The alpha gulps, his hand wrapped around his neck.

Hysterical laughter bubbles out of me.

Chapter Seventeen

"This way." Leo steers me in the opposite direction from where I bolted down a long hallway.

Moving as fast as I can without making too much noise, I strain my ears in hopes to hear where the others are. A soul-crushing screech comes from somewhere behind us, and I jerk to a stop while the alpha plows into my back. I try to sidestep him, but he grabs my upper arm, tugging me along.

"That's probably Tenebris." Reaching a corner, he sticks his head out fast before doing it a second time slowly, making sure no one is going to jump us. "We don't want to be where he is right now."

"Right." Adrenaline is still pumping through my veins and I haven't accepted the fact that Alexius is dead. Not really. Although his head in my hands is playing behind my eyelids on repeat every time I blink.

Leo opens each door we pass but all of them are empty. That's until he finds a locked one that he does his best to break through with no luck. It takes me a moment to see that this room actually has a window next to it. Well, not a window, but a glass part of the wall allowing you to see inside it. Leaving the alpha to continue banging up his shoulder on the door—because why not, right—I move in front of the glass and stare inside the room.

"She's not there," I tell Leo, but I can't look away.

"How do you know?" He grunts, then slams his body in the door again, making the glass rattle and the walls groan.

"I see that she's not there." That gets his attention and he glares at me, rubbing his shoulder.

"You could've said something sooner." The mutt is cute when he pouts but I don't dare tell him that right now.

"Whoever is in there, it's a male." I point with a jerk of my chin and Leo comes to stand next to me.

It's another sterile room but this one has a few machines and a metal bed inside it. A male is laid out on it, but I can only see his feet and his chest because the rest of his body is covered with a sheet. All the machines are connected to him and blinking. I assume they are beeping, too, since no sound can be heard through the glass.

"We should get him out," Leo mumbles next to me, but something inside me flipflops at the idea for some reason.

"Later." Since I can't figure out if the feeling is good or bad, I'd rather get my mother out first before attempting another rescue.

"Very well." He follows after me, but I can see from the corner of my eye that he is watching me warily.

"Your skin and hair changed, you know," he pipes in conversationally before I can ask him what's wrong.

"What?" My feet slow down but Leo doesn't have time to answer.

A hunter barrels towards us from another hallway, a second one right on his heels. The alpha and I split apart, him moving a foot or so ahead to give us both room. I wince when the first hunter smacks right into him and both of them hit the wall, plaster raining over their heads. The second hunter jumps a couple feet in the air, lifting his knee at chest level before he sails at me. Reaching up, I grab him by the raised leg and one hip, twisting to throw him down the hallway. Agile like a cat, he lands on his feet and bounces right back at me. I repeat the same thing again, throwing him on the other side with the same result. At least it seems they don't have any weapons.

"Stop playing with him, Drake," Leo snarls, his fingernails lengthening as he opens up the hunter's chest like a can of soup. Dark red, almost black, paints the hunter's clothing, spreading like an oil spill down his body.

The second hunter bounces at me, taking us both down. My head hits the tiled floor with a crack that rattles my brain enough to snap me out of whatever is clouding it. Throwing an elbow in his gut, I flip around, taking hold of his head and twisting. The head pops out like a cherry, blood spraying from his neck and messing up the ground. Alexius's face flashes before my eyes and I throw the head away like it burned me as I jump to my feet.

"I see a pattern." Leo snickers, kicking at the dead hunter sprawled at his feet.

"Yeah, me too." Not looking at him, I move down the hallway.

The shock is wearing off and I'm starting to get dizzy. Internally, I'm freaking that I ripped someone's head off without blinking an eye, but you'd never know from looking at me. My movements are so fluid and calm you'd think I'm out for a stroll. I hear the banging before I reach the door. I don't need to hear it to know it's my mother. Steeling my spine, I wrench the door handle with all I've got until it pops open with a hiss. Leo whistles low slinking closer to peek over my shoulder.

I push the door open, stepping inside.

"Francesca Drake." My mother's voice grinds on all my nerve endings. "I knew you were an insolent child, but I never knew you were this stupid."

"Good to see you too, Mother. I'm happy to see that you are unharmed." Leo walks in warily behind me. "Leo, meet my mother, Sophia. Mother, this is Leo, my friend."

Huffing incredulously, she gives the alpha a once over, making him shuffle on his feet. "Friend," she says it like it's a curse.

"Can we please get out of here?" With a quick glance around the room, I see that she isn't hurt. Well, she isn't bleeding at least.

"First I want to find that insufferable male to give him a piece of my mind." Folding her arms under her breasts, she sniffs. "He thinks just because he can lock me in this room that I'm not going to rip into him."

"I'm assuming you are talking about Alex?" I see Leo widening his eyes comically.

"I do not know his name, Francesca. You don't exchange pleasantries with your kidnappers," she tells me like I'm a simpleton and need it explained.

Pinching the bridge of my nose, I breathe in deeply. "He is dead, Mother."

"You can't possibly ..."

"I killed him," I deadpan, waving my hands at my blood-soaked clothing and cutting her off. She looks at me dubiously but thankfully doesn't comment.

"We are all clear." Zoltan's voice coming from behind Leo speeds up my heart until I see my mother turn her full attention on him. Then it jackhammers for a different reason.

"And who might you be?" Her arms unfold, her hands smoothing down her clothing while she bats her eyelashes at the Daywalker.

"That's Zoltan." Closing my eyes, I pray for patience. "Another ... friend."

"For an awkward creature, you've sure made a lot of friends." She's not taking her eyes off him, and I grind my teeth.

"He is a Daywalker." I have no idea what possesses me to say it.

My mother jerks back like she's been slapped, her mouth moving like a carp out of water. Groaning, I clench my fists but it's too late now to take the words back. Very slowly, I turn to face Zoltan and a lump forms in my throat. His blue gaze is intently focused on me, his shoulders hunching slightly as if he will walk up to me. My mother hisses, jumping between us and breaking the spell.

Zoltan scowls at his feet.

"Don't you dare touch her with your filthy hands, Daywalker." Hissing at him, she even lifts her hands, fingers curled into makeshift claws at his face. "You'll have to go through me first. Francesca, step back child."

Leo looks like he swallowed a lemon.

"Zoltan, meet my mother Sophia," I grumble, wishing the ground would open so I could jump in the hole and disappear. "Mother, this is Zoltan. He helped me come rescue you."

"Pleasure to meet you, Mrs. Drake." Inclining his head, the vampire looks from me to my mother and back. If only I can read his mind to know what he is thinking.

"You fornicate with Daywalkers now?" She turns on me

with murder on her face. "What in the fates name is the matter with you girl."

I've had enough.

"Are you going to move so we can leave this damn place, or should I leave you to find your own way home … Mother?" Squaring my shoulders, I frown at her.

"You … you …" she stutters, lost for words.

"I thought so." Moving around her, I stride to the door. Zoltan has to move so I don't smack into him. "Move along then. We don't have time to linger for your tantrums."

We all shift like a wave, falling in step with each other. I can feel the heat of Zoltan's body at my back, just as I can feel my mother's glare drilling holes in the back of my skull. Leo, on the other hand, I can hear clearly. He is clearing his throat, coughing. and choking so he doesn't laugh. Unfortunately, I find nothing funny at the moment.

"We can't leave yet." My mother's desperate outburst jerks me to a stop, so I look at her over my shoulder. "Not without …" Gulping air, she twists her fingers in front of her. "Not without your brother." The words are tangled together.

"Nice try." My mouth hurts from pressing it too tight. "I don't have a brother," I tell the two males that look shell-shocked. "Any other bullshit you want to say to stall?"

"It's true." When her breath shutters, I feel like someone just ripped my heart out of my chest.

"Father never said …"

"He has a different father, but he is still your brother." Her chin kicks up, daring me to say something.

Oh, I fucking dare. I dare a lot.

"And you accuse me of fornicating?" Getting in her face should've made her back away, but she stiffens her spine.

"He is half human. You cannot leave him in the hands

of these monsters. Have you no heart?" That last part is a sob and I shrivel inside, until the look in her eyes hardens. "They got him because of you."

Closing my eyes, I pretend it doesn't hurt that she always finds something to tell me I'm nothing or unworthy. Anything to say that once in her life she didn't regret having me. I come up empty. A stray thought pops in my head, making me wonder if I was the one tied to machines, would she stop to save me?

My eyes snap open.

"Fuck!" Spinning around, I bolt back the way we came, sliding in the blood from the dead hunters Leo and I killed, ramming my hip and shoulder in the wall. I can hear Leo jabbering behind, explaining fast to them why I reacted the way I did. Zoltan's beating footsteps catch up to me just as I reach the room with the glass wall. I have no idea what those machines are, but they are definitely not good since they are connected to Roberti and Alexius. I rattle the door-knob, but my sweaty palm slides off it, making me scream in fury.

Zoltan shoves me away and barrels through the wall instead of the door like it's made of paper. White dust and plaster rains down on him, turning him all white like a ghost. I have no time to think about anything but the male on that metal bed. Sprinting, I skid to a stop when I'm standing right above him.

"No," I whisper through numb lips.

All the air is pushed out of my lungs and the ground disappears from under my feet. I feel myself going down and I tense, expecting the impact to hurt since I can't stop the fall. Strong familiar arms wrap around me, one under my knees and the other around my back, lifting me to a firm chest. Zoltan's nearness is the only thing keeping me sane at this moment.

"Francesca?" Zoltan says my name softly like a question. I can hear his heart pounding in his chest as his arms tighten around me.

"I know him." Looking up at his face, I see him frown. "I saw him the first time you took me to the human realm. He stopped trying to get me to go with him and not to the portal. I think ..." Swallowing thickly, it takes two tries to finish the sentence. "I think he knew they were waiting for us."

"Oh, no," my mother breathes.

Chapter Eighteen

"You guys have to see this!" Daren skids down the hall, missing the open door before sticking his head back inside the room.

The beeping of the machines drills holes into my pounding temples. I press myself closer to Zoltan's chest like I can make myself merge with him, like I can disappear for a little while. The Daywalker turns his body to the side so he can see the mage who is staring wide eyed at all of us gathered around the bed with my brother's unmoving body stretched out on it.

My brother.

The thought dunks my head into deafening silence, like I'm drifting in an abyss with just intervals of static bursting through here and there. How did my life get messed up so fast? Although I complained all the time and lived with a crippling fear each day that someone will find out what I am and kill me … life was actually not that bad. Now there's some new revelation every day that digs my grave deeper than the day before. Eventually, it'll be a bottomless pit where not even my soul will be able to find a way out.

"What did you find?" Zoltan's deep voice vibrates through his chest under my ear, calming me more than it should.

"You can stand on your own feet," my mother hisses under her breath, watching Zoltan like he is a venomous snake.

"If I told you, you wouldn't believe me. You've got to come see." Daren pushes off the door, walking in cautiously and stealing quick glances at my brother. "Who's that? One of ours?"

"Francesca's brother." Leo stares the mage down intently as if daring him to say something about that little bomb dropping.

A quick look passes between my mother and Daren, and I just know without asking. Daren knew about this, just like he was obviously having secret conversations with my father about me. What else will tonight bring? Is my dead father coming out of his grave? Will I grow a second head? At the rate things are going, anything is possible. A hollow, humorless laugh comes from me, and every head in the room turns my way.

"Can we remove the machines without hurting him?" With great reluctance, I wiggle out of Zoltan's arms and he lowers my feet to the ground but doesn't remove his hand from my shoulder. "Before I lose my shit with all the crazy here, I'd like to go home." Another crazy laugh bursts through my lips. "Home. What a fucking joke."

"Francesca Drake, language," my mother snaps, and I round on her.

"You want fucking language, Mother?" She takes a step back, her eyes bulging out at my animosity, but I'm way past caring. "How many different species did you fuck without finding it important to tell me about it? Are there more children scattered around the human realm? Sienna? And you dare lecture me about fornicating?" My entire body is vibrating in anger. "It's called fucking, Mother! At least I don't pop out children left and right."

"Francesca." Zoltan pulls me back to his chest, tightening an arm around my waist. "I know you are angry, I'm furious on your behalf, but we can't do this here. We cleared the hunters but it's still not safe. Let us go, love."

That last word is the only thing that penetrates the red haze that is blurring my vision. My mother's mouth drops open comically and I would've laughed if I myself wasn't shocked speechless. Very slowly, I turn in Zoltan's arms while searching his face for any indication that he's used it to manipulate me into calming down. Or by a mistake. My hands lift to his chest, my fingers trembling from all the emotions swirling inside me when I see that he has removed the mask of indifference he's had after my stupid behavior. He gives me a small smile that weakens my knees, pulling me closer to him.

The clearing of a throat jerks my eyes around the room and my face heats in embarrassment. Leo offers a quick grin, winking conspiratorially at me. I thump my forehead on Zoltan's chest. The vampire's hand glides up and down my back, melting me against him, but I'm aware that all eyes are on me. Well, maybe not all, but the three males and my mother. That is enough to pull me out of the mushy feelings messing with my head. If Zoltan has forgiven me, we can talk about it after we are out of this place.

"Where is Astara? Fenrir?" Stepping away so I can think straight without Zoltan's sinful scent filling my nostrils, my eyes fall on the alpha, because I'm refusing to ask Daren the traitor anything. "Tenebris? You said they are alive."

"We secured the other part of the building." Daren seems a little pale, his green eyes a touch too fevered and too wide. "They stayed to keep guard until I get the rest of you. We weren't sure if Sophia was in any state to walk around." When I raise my eyebrow, he blushes furiously. "If she's been hurt, I mean."

"Let's hope she's not pregnant." The words are out before I can stop them.

"How dare you." The tone of voice my mother uses is one I'm very familiar with. Involuntarily I flinch, hating myself for it.

"Can we move him, or should we just take everything with us?" Thankfully Leo changes the subject, which saves me from continuing the argument with my mother in front of everyone.

"Do we know what any of this is?" Moving closer to the bed, I stare at the sleeping face of my brother. "Is he sedated or in a coma?" An idea occurs to me, so I look at Zoltan over my shoulder. "Can you use your mind f—your mind power to force him awake?"

"I can try." His lips quirk on one corner at my slip up. "I'm hesitant, though. What if they pumped him full of something that will harm him if we wake him too quickly?"

"I really think you should see what we found before you do anything." Daren sighs, rubbing a hand over his face. "Fuck. This changes everything."

"I will stay with him," my mother says softly, reaching for my brother's hand when it becomes obvious I'm not sure what to do.

"You should see it too, Franky." Daren is already walking out, leaving us the option to follow him or not.

With a nod at my mother, I hurry after Daren, and Zoltan and Leo are right behind me. All sorts of thoughts and scenarios are playing in my head, from mutilated bodies to summoning rituals being performed here. I wouldn't put any of it past Roberti. My brother's handsome face floats to the front of my mind, his voice begging me to go with him and not to the portal. Would he have told me who he was? Did he know who I was at the time? Too many questions and not enough answers. For every answer I find, more questions pop up.

"You okay?" Zoltan takes my hand, slowing me down just as Leo moves around me and jogs ahead to catch up to Daren.

"I'm not sure." Releasing a shuddering sigh, I lace my fingers through his and hold my breath to see what he will do.

"We will figure it out." Giving me a reassuring squeeze, he wiggles our hold to make our hands fit together better. In my uncertainty, I am gripping only the tips of his fingers, making it awkward. "This place looks like a storage facility for whatever they are doing."

"You mean apart from holding hostages?"

"That, too." He chuckles. "Your mother really is something."

"No kidding." Not wanting to discuss my mother right now while I'm still angry with her, I blurt out what's been bothering me since I found out I have a sibling. "You think they knew he was my brother and that was why they took him? Alex wasn't sure he had my mother here, and that was how I tricked him into leaving the room so I could free myself. Roberti hasn't been here to confirm it. So how would he know about my brother when I didn't even know I had one."

"I cannot say, Francesca." Taking the left curve of the hallway, Zoltan rubs his chin. "You coming to the academy uncovered an entire organization functioning under our noses. We knew about the hunters, but we were clueless that our own were the head of that slippery snake."

"I still don't think Roberti is the mastermind behind it all." The voices of the others reach my ears, coming from the open double doors near the end of the hall. Roaring cries of the panther can be heard through the sound. "He is power hungry and arrogant for sure, but to want to destroy Sienna? The place he lorded over for so long? Someone else is pulling the strings and they promised him something better, otherwise he would've never given up the influence he already had."

"You think they promised him the human realm?" Zoltan sounds doubtful. "He will need an army of at least a hundred times the number of hunters in this world to take control of it."

"Even with a Titan on his side?" I tilt my head to see him better and he flashes his fangs at me.

"Especially if he frees a Titan. No one in the human realm can control those, of that I'm sure."

"Not even you?" His smile grows at my question, sending my pulse into overdrive.

"I'm not from the human realm." He winks and I almost trip over my feet.

We reach the double doors, so I regain my balance with a hand on the doorframe. The implications of what the vampire said are running through my head, making me dizzy and it takes me a long moment to understand what I'm looking at. Zoltan stiffens and his fingers tighten on mine painfully, confusing me even more. Astara, Leo, Daren, and Fenrir are standing in the middle of the large space that stretches before my eyes. Tenebris is pacing close to the doors like a guard, his face twisted in a snarl and sounds like cries, roars, and purrs mixed together are coming out of him without a pause. His smooth black fur is charred in a few patches, the hairs sticking out with no shine to them. Behind them all, rows and rows of metal cabinets with glass doors are lined up as far as my eyes can see. In the closest one, clearly visible, are bags of blood hanging on little hooks attached to the top of each shelf. The first cabinet is also open, one bag of blood missing from it. When my gaze swings to the people clustered in the middle of the room, I see it in Astara's hand. My friend also looks green in the face like she's about to puke.

"I don't get it." I jump out of my skin when Tenebris shrieks at me. "Shut up cat! We knew they were dealing with blood, so why is this so shocking?" Looking away from the grim faces, I turn to Zoltan. "What am I missing?"

"Human?" He doesn't look at me, instead addresses his sister.

Astara shakes her head then winces, pressing a hand to her stomach. "It's synthetic." Her voice is hoarse like she's been screaming. "Lucky Daren was here to purge it out of me because I can still feel remnants of it."

Releasing my hand, Zoltan walks to his sister, his long legs eating the space with heavy thumps of his boots. It's always fascinating to watch him walk. Every time his foot touches the ground it's like him telling the earth it should bow to him and be grateful for having his weight on it. Snatching the bag from Astara's hand, he brings it to his nose, jerking it away the same second.

"What in the fates name is this?" The vampire glares at the bag, his face twisted in disgust.

"I can't be one-hundred percent sure until I confirm

with one of our medics but I think it's a mixture of multiple species in one." Fenrir doesn't sound like himself, and I notice him holding his ribs on the left side while favoring that leg too.

"They are making super blood?" I snort because it sounds ridiculous saying it out loud.

"No." Daren rushes to a corner of the room I can't see from the door, grabbing a folder and bringing it to Zoltan. "It's worse than that."

My feet move on their own, curious to see what Daren has found. The folder is open between Zoltan's hands and he flicks pages fast, then his movements slow. His head lifts as he locks eyes with Fenrir before returning his attention to the pages. When I reach him, I lean on his arm, sticking my head over it to see what problem we will be facing now. My blood curdles in my veins.

"They didn't know he was your brother," Zoltan tells me, not taking his eyes off the pages. "They search for half-bloods then feed them the synthetic blood of mixed species, creating a new generation of hunters with all the qualities of the species but none of the setbacks. The strongest predators they can find to unleash on Sienna and on the humans."

"Like super hunters?" I can barely hear from the buzzing in my ears, but hanging on his arm to stay standing, Zoltan's words come loud and clear.

"Like perfect hunters."

Chapter Nineteen

"Easy there." Reaching for the agitated Tenebris, I yank my hand back when he snaps his jaws an inch from my fingers. "Are you sure I'm the one that can calm him down? He doesn't seem particularly happy to have me near him."

"I'm sure." Fenrir doesn't look like he is sure at all, which makes my heart somersault in my chest. "Something in the blood made him wilder than he already was. He tore into the first bags when we opened the cabinets."

Now that he mentions it, I can see a few blood bags missing from the lower shelves through the open glass doors. The panther's ears are pinned back, and his chest lowers to the floor, his piercing gaze locked on me and those fangs the size of my forearm bared in a warning. I gulp down my fear and decide a different approach is needed if we ever want to leave this place. Either not in one piece, or not with the feline.

"Stop that you stupid cat!" Lifting to my full height, I bark at him. "You think any of us like this? Get yourself together so we can find out what's going on. Do it now, Tenebris!"

His eyes narrow on my face, so I return the hostile glare with one of my own. Knowing full well he can sense my fear, I mentally nudge the entity inside me and ask for help. I haven't done this consciously until now, so I'm shocked when it eagerly answers, uncoiling the power in my chest with a flourish. My view shifts and colors burst to life, everything around me becoming clearer and more beautiful.

"Oh, shit." Astara breathes, moving slightly away from where Tenebris and I are facing off.

The creature inside me preens at having its ego stroked with the fact she recognizes the superiority. It's a ridiculous feeling to have, but it fills every inch of my body as I watch Tenebris arch his back, bristling. There is also a horrifying sound coming from behind me and it's raising the hairs on my neck, but I don't look away from the intent emerald gaze of the panther. It takes a few long moments before my power wafts out of me in waves, slapping Tenebris in the face each time the heat bursts around us. With a very pitiful sound, the panther ducks his head, lowers his eyes, and slinks closer, nudging it under my hand.

I wrestle the magic into submission with great effort, the beads of sweat trickling down my spine and making me tremble like a leaf. Blowing out a breath, my shoulders sag and I sink my fingers in the silky fur on Tenebris's head and neck, the large feline wrapping around me so close he almost pushes me on the ground. That's when I notice his body is shivering as well.

"It's okay." Blood is rushing through my ears, tightening my hold on the coarse hairs. "It'll be okay." Whispering reassurances more to myself than the feline shifter, I look around us and my heart does a painful jerk in my chest.

Zoltan is crouched behind me, fangs bared and eyes glowing as bright as two suns on his handsome face. He's more terrifying than handsome at the moment, but there is nothing that isn't breathtaking about the male. Every muscle in his body is coiled and ready to spring into action. I guess the sound that raised the hairs on my neck came from him. It's a good thing I didn't see him like that because I have a bad feeling the entity inside me would've loved the challenge this particular predator represents.

"Sorry." I snicker like an idiot, well aware it's my power blasting him that brings his instincts to the surface. "I couldn't think of another way to calm the cat down."

"I must say, Franky, that your methods, although effective, will make us start attacking each other if you don't give us a warning." It's strange to hear the strain in Daren's voice, and I notice the sparks of tiny flames dancing around his fingertips.

"I need a moment." Zoltan's voice is so deep it sends a thrill rushing through every inch of my body.

"Can't you try and purge whatever poison they gave my brother like you did with Astara?" Allowing the vampire time to bring himself under control, I give him my back.

Daren's eyes bulge out, as if my gaze should be on Zoltan's in case he is ready to attack again. But I trust him, and that surprises me since he did almost choke me to death earlier this evening.

"I can try but I didn't sense it in him like I did with her." The mage flicks his eyes between me and Zoltan, unwilling to look away from the fang-baring vampire as easily as I do. "I healed Fenrir and Tenebris as well, so I'm not at my full strength." He rubs his face, fatigue lining his features. "I'll feel better if Aspen checks him out."

"You know Aspen?" The mention of the redhead medic

that verbally slapped Leo and Fenrir makes me wonder just how much Daren is in the know about the comings and goings in the academy. "Let me guess, another relative of yours? It seems to me your bloodline is as neck deep in this clusterfuck as mine."

"No." Color creeps into his cheeks, and my eyebrows crawl up to my hairline. "Just an acquaintance. She is one of the best medics I know." He hurries to assure me like I would doubt her ability just because they may have tangled under the sheets.

"What are we going to do with all this?" Now that there is no one to kill and nothing to help wake my brother up, I want to be out of here as soon as possible.

"Destroy it," Fenrir says with so much passion packed in his voice I have to do a double take.

"You sure you are well?" The fact that he doesn't react in any way at the mention of me having a brother is not lost on me, but I have no energy left to dwell on it.

On anything really.

"I'm as good as I can be given everything that's happened." The Fae's shoulders snap back, and he stands taller under my scrutiny. "Let's take everyone out and set this place ablaze." An eager glint enters his gaze.

"I'll get Sophia and your brother." Leo is already jogging out of the room. "Meet you outside." He disappears through the doors before I can stop him.

"We need some of the blood to take with us." Astara is looking much better; the color has returned in her face although she still seems unsteady on her feet.

"You'll be able to destroy this place and open a portal?" Watching Astara fill her arms with bags, I can't help but ask the mage if he is up to the task. "You look like you can barely stand on your feet."

"I'll do it." Cracking his neck, he shakes his hands off, still eyeing Zoltan warily. "Only one portal though, so we all go together."

"I'm ready." Astara comes back.

She has pulled her shirt up, making a pouch from it on her belly and filled it with blood bags to bursting. The liquid sloshes around the plastic holding it with each step she takes, and I can't take my eyes off it. Just how messed up are these people to go to such lengths? There can't be that many half-bloods for all the blood they have stored in this place. And is this the only building filled with it or are there others. If so, how many more.

My headache returns with a vengeance.

"Let us go." Zoltan wraps an arm around my shoulders, tucking me under his arm.

"Better?" I turn to him, seeing his jaw clenched and a muscle jumping in it.

"Well enough." He looks down at me, his gaze dancing all over my face. "I didn't expect you to control your powers so well. It took me by surprise."

"I've never tried it like this before." Gnawing on my lip, I see his eyes zero in on it. "It comes easily when it wants to answer. I'm not sure I can do it anytime I want … yet."

"We'll figure it out, just like everything else." With one glance at Tenebris he moves me towards the doors.

The panther doesn't leave my side, making it difficult to walk without bouncing between him and Zoltan's body. My skin is pebbled from the sloshing sound the bags make behind me, so I grind my teeth and keep my eyes in front of me. I don't even want to look at the hallways we are passing. Without the adrenaline rush or the fear for our lives, everything looks tainted and disgusting. It's sterile and white, just like the uniforms the hunters prefer. Void of anything.

Void of life.

"Just a minute longer," Zoltan grumbles under his breath when I shiver in his arms.

I see Leo standing at the bent-and-twisted front gates of this facility, my mother clutching the rail on the bed where my brother is still lying unconscious. The thought of a sibling has never occurred to me. Worrying about my own life had been enough for me, and I'm not sure I would've been able to fear for another person on top of that. But I'd be lying to myself if I said that knowing about him hasn't already taken roots in my heart. He might be a stranger to me, but already my protective instincts are burning in my chest. I want to kill anyone that hurt him.

"We need to move a ways out so I can burn it down." Daren doesn't slow down when we reach my mother and the alpha. "We didn't search good enough, and there might be all sorts of things inside it."

"Shouldn't we look to see if we can find anything useful?" I ask Fenrir because he is being unusually quiet. I'm not sure it's from the injury, either. The Fae heals faster than anyone I know, apart from Zoltan.

"We have enough." He looks my way then winces, grabbing his ribs again. "As soon as we get back, I'm dispatching teams to search all other addresses we found around the perimeter of the base Roberti had. If there is anything useful, we will find it. There is nothing we need from this one."

I skid to a stop when he says that, ducking under Zoltan's arm. "I'll be right back."

Not waiting to hear if they are okay with me going back, I bolt inside the building. My boots are thumping a staccato on the tiled floors through the hallways, sliding on the pools of blood spilled all over the place. Jumping over bodies and body parts where Tenebris must've been having a blast playing with the hunters, I run for all I'm worth.

I miss the correct hallway twice before I finally reach the familiar door. With my heart in my throat, I push my way inside the room where Alexius had me tied up, my eyes zeroing in on his headless body immediately. Not wanting to waste time, I find his head tossed in the far-left corner and, snatching it up by the hair, I swallow the bile burning my throat. Turning around, I shriek and drop the head with a wet plop at my feet.

Tenebris is standing at the open door watching me with a glittering gaze. I didn't hear him follow me and he scared the shit out of me, his black coat standing out stark among all the white around us. Pushing the hair off my face, I bend down and grab the head again. The panther looks smug at my reaction and snorts. At least he is not trying to bite my head off right now. Speaking of heads, I'm ignoring the one dangling from my hand as I push past Tenebris. He sniffs at it, growling unhappily even though he follows next to me as we make our way out.

Zoltan meets us just as we turn the first corner. The vampire followed as well and my stupid heart melts knowing he didn't want me alone in this damn place. I lift the head like an offering in his face.

"Will this work for the oath?" The thought hits me when Fenrir said there was nothing we can use. "The Board should be pleased I'm bringing them the head of the traitor, right?"

"No." His lips press in a thin line. "But no harm in trying." He spins on his heel, falling in step with me. "I still don't think you should take the oath. If you have made up your mind to go with it, I can be persuasive to make it enough."

"I knew there was a reason to keep you around." As soon as I say it, I wince remembering the argument we had. "Too soon?"

"A little." Chuckling, he bumps his shoulder into mine. "There is a long conversation you and I are going to have. Let us deal with this first."

The expressions on the faces of Astara and Fenrir may be comical if not for the head I'm holding like a plastic bag as it brushes against my thigh. The Fae grins at me but there is no humor in it. Just some gleeful satisfaction of seeing the one that betrayed them pay for his actions. Astara, on the other hand, is undecided if she wants to be impressed or disgusted. She settles on firm determination and gives me a nod that I return. By the time we are done with Roberti, I'm not sure our friendships and the way we see each other will ever be the same.

"Half way down the block should suffice." Daren walks through the gates with the rest of us behind him.

"Francesca?" my mother calls my name to get my attention, but I can't deal with whatever she has to say to me right now. All I can do is walk while pretending I'm not swinging a head like some headless horseman through the streets of the human realm.

"This should be enough." Daren stops, turning to face the facility while glowing like a beacon of hope with lights blazing.

It's a good thing it's not fully morning yet. Dark clouds are stuffing the sky above our heads like cotton balls pushed together. Pale grayish rays are forcing their way through and piercing the gloomy weather, but the light isn't enough to be harmful to my eyes. A crack of lightning sounds far ahead, the ozone in the air burning my nose hairs with each breath I take.

"Is this you?" I flick a glance at the mage.

"No, it's the weather." Frustration tightens his face as he lifts his hands in front of him.

We all watch in fascination when that burning lava magic swirls between his palms. It grows larger with each blink, twisting and turning like a bag full of snakes. The heat from it is searing my skin so instinctively I move away from it, bumping into Zoltan who is back to being my shadow. The thought warms the chill that is occupying my chest. Muttering something in a language I don't understand, Daren flings his hands in front of him and sends the magic at the facility with incredible speed. The bubbling lava bathes everything red as it sails down the street, disappearing through the destroyed gates. Silence follows, but it only lasts a split second even though it feels like an eternity while we all hold our breaths.

A blast that shoves me back a few steps is followed by an inferno reaching for the gray clouds. I shield my face with my arm, the fires spreading around the large building and blistering my skin like I'm standing next to the sun. The others are shouting something, and Zoltan curls around me like a protective bubble, but I can't look away from the sight in front of me. Just how powerful is Daren? I never stopped long enough to ask that question.

"Shit." Astara's voice comes so close to my ear I can feel her breath on my skin. She must've covered me on the other side opposite her brother. "Open the portal, Daren," she shouts, the squishy bags of blood wobbling between us.

"I'm trying," Daren barks, his voice strained now more than ever. "Fuck! I'm trying." The last word is pushed out through grated teeth.

"Let us move closer." Zoltan nudges the four of us,

Tenebris twisted between all our legs where the mage is standing with the bed, my mother and Fenrir at his back.

We waddle to join them, and I watch the portal start sparkling, spitting bursts of light like fireworks amid the inferno its facing. It's slow moving, every second a painful reminder that if he doesn't open it fast, we will burn to a crisp along with the cursed facility. Disgusting or not, I shove the head between our bodies to protect the identity, at least enough to satisfy the old jerks when I throw it at their faces. Imagining the looks they'll wear makes it easier to deal with my skin melting off my bones.

The portal bursts open.

"Go, go, go," Leo chants, the gateway stretching like a bubble, reflecting the fires that are trying to reach the sky.

Fenrir grabs my mother with one hand and the bed with my brother with the other, yanking them hard enough that the muscles on his back are jumping from the strain. With a pained shout, all three of them disappear, my heart twisting from knowing the Fae is suffering to protect my family. Zoltan gives us a hard push and my stomach drops to my feet when I lose the ground. We all sail through the air before hitting the center of the portal. At the last moment my arm snaps out, taking hold of Daren's shirt and yanking him with us.

"Thank fu …" My sigh is cut off by barked commands, snarls, and furious growling.

"Perfect timing, Ms. Drake." Silas sneers.

I blink fast until I can clearly see his ugly mug.

The head drops from my numb fingers.

Chapter Twenty

We are all in the dining hall that has been emptied to wait for our arrival. At least that's my guess as to why it's empty. All the tables, chairs, and furniture are pushed to the sides, making it look abandoned and hollow. Zoltan is sprawled at my feet, Alexius's head perched next to his face like a lover. Astara is suspended in the air, held up by an invisible force with the blood bags still twitching on the floor under her where she dropped them. My head jerks to the side seeing Leo, Daren, and Fenrir also unconscious, and my blood curdles in my veins, numbing me. Tenebris is motionless on his side, but at least his eyes are open and burning with rage.

The Board is standing around us looking smug as shit about incapacitating the three males and the shifter who would've ripped their heads off if they were still standing, the old mage twirling the magic he used on them between his hands. I love that they still underestimate a female. My mother's gasps are like daggers in my brain.

I grin like a fiend at them.

"Look at you three," I chirp cheerfully. "A welcoming committee. I must say it suits you."

"You must give the oath, Ms. Drake." Daren's father looks down his nose at me. "We can't wait for you to explore the realms first. The safety of the academy and Sienna is first and foremost."

"Explore?" Deadpanning, I glare at them. "I brought you a gift." Kicking the head with my toes, I watch it roll until it stops at their feet. "That ought to be considered a present from my vacations."

"Alexius got what he deserved." Silas sniffs, unimpressed. "That doesn't negate the fact the oath must take a place."

"And you thought, 'hey, let's hurt those she cares about and blackmail her into it' because that always works like a charm, huh?" Clenching my fists, I prod at the entity inside me, mentally hoping she'll come to my aid again.

The bitch purrs.

"It's not difficult to do Ms. Drake. All you have to do is drink from the chalice." The old shifter waves a silver cup at me, brandishing it like a sword in my face. "The magic of this place will do the rest. It's part of you, isn't it? Soren made sure of that. You can't possibly ask all of us to trust you when you obviously don't trust yourself."

I bite my tongue to stop all the words standing on the tip of it that I want to throw at them. Talk about shitty timing. The old fools couldn't give me at least an hour to take my brother to medic Aspen and my mother out of here. I wish they would knock her out too, so she doesn't see this clusterfuck. It'll be one more thing in her arsenal that she'll use to remind me what kind of a mistake I am, I'm sure.

"I need to take my mother back where she belongs." There you go, no one said I can't negotiate. "I said I will take the oath and I haven't changed my mind. Let the others go, and they won't influence my decision. This is between you and me."

Silas is already shaking his head and I'm not even done talking. There is a glint in their gazes, telling me they have no doubt in their minds that they've won. I, on the other hand, think if I stall enough Zoltan and Fenrir will break through whatever magic they used on them. I will enjoy sitting on the sidelines while the Board is being slapped around. Just like everything else in my life, this is not as easy as that.

"You take the oath, now," Daren's father snaps impatiently.

"How did you manage to knock them out?" Gingerly, I step over Zoltan moving closer to the dumbasses. "That's some strong juju you are packing." I flick my gaze to the mage.

"The academy's magic knows this needs to be done. It helped." Silas stupidly gloats, unaware he just warned me that I can't count on the entity inside me for aid. No wonder the bitch purrs.

"Of course, it did." Mumbling, I inch closer without being too obvious about it.

A crazy thought flicks through my mind that Soren is in on this, that maybe this is just one more hook he is trying to sink into me, but I push it away. I'll deal with the ancient Fae when I fix this shitstorm. I'll drag him out of that bed by his feet if I have to.

"It'll take but a moment, Ms. Drake, and then you can continue whatever it is you were doing." Daren's father softens his words like that will make me jump at the opportunity they are offering. He really must think I'm dumb.

But what choice do I have?

I've already decided to go along with this insanity, much to Zoltan's and Fenrir's dismay and protests. They both have taken the oath and they seem perfectly fine, even have their own minds still. They still know right from wrong too. If they were brainwashed, I would've fought against it like a wounded animal. But now? Remembering Astara telling me about Zoltan's sacrifice is still not enough to change my mind. I want the assholes off my back, and the fates never gave me the option of having a true mate. I guess that means it can't be taken from me.

My eyes go to the top of Zoltan's head on their own. No matter how hard I fight against my feelings for him, nothing stops them. No, they only burn stronger the more I force myself to push him away. They muddle my mind and cripple me in situations where I need a clear head. Yet, there they are, churning and stretching, occupying every inch of my soul. If this is how he makes me feel now, I don't want the true-mate connection, even if it is on the table for my taking. From what I've heard it's all-consuming. *Like this is not.* The voice in my head snorts at me.

"This can't wait why exactly?" My feet slide closer to the old mage.

"There is no time like the present," the shifter says cheerfully, tugging on the shirt he is wearing and folding it up to his elbow.

What does he think? We will wrestle?

"Very well." My mother screams a high-pitched sound when I bounce from the balls of my feet, body slamming the old mage.

We topple together, taking the shifter to the ground with us, the silver chalice tinkling happily on the tiled floors. I lose sight of it, elbowing my way up and hitting a nose with a sickening crunch. A neck gives way at my jabs. Silas dances away like a fucking ballerina, and it pisses me off that he isn't on the ground, too. Growls and snarls come from the two board members while I punch and kick every part of them I can reach. The old vampire moves closer before jumping back and looking for an opening to help them break up our brawl.

My mother's terrified scream drains all the fight from me.

"Step away from them," Silas snarls, spittle dangling from his lips when I look at him.

"Take your filthy hands off me." My mother swings a fist, backhanding Silas and breaking his nose.

His grip on her hair doesn't loosen, but it's beautiful to watch the blood flow down his mouth and soak into his shirt. He wrenches her head to the side, bearing his fangs. I jump to my feet instantly, stepping away from the two still in a pile of twisted limbs on the ground. Lifting both hands palms up, I move further away not taking my eyes off him. The mage and the shifter are cursing up a storm while pushing to their feet.

"The chalice." Silas jerks his chin and the old shifter scrambles up, rushing to grab it where it rolled next to Tenebris. The panther snarls viciously but not a muscle twitches on his body.

I stand frozen just like my mother, whose eyes are burning with anger. We watch the old shifter slashing his wrist. He dribbles his blood in the chalice, pushing acid to flood my mouth. Breathing through my nose, I try my best not to vomit. The Board member walks up to Silas doing the same thing, and green smoke swirls out of the silver cup when their blood combines. The mage is the last, the green puffs flowing freely over the rim of the chalice with his life fluid added to the mix.

"Just a sip, Ms. Drake." The shifter brings it to me like an offering. "It'll be over before you know it and none of this needs to happen again.

Silas's and Daren's father are chanting things in a foreign language, and bile rises to the roof of my mouth while goosebumps erupt all over my skin. I wish I was like Fenrir and can understand all these exotic tongues so I know if they are cursing me to all eternity. All I can do now is look around at everyone I care about unconscious and my mother's freaked-out face like she's the one that needs to drink that gunk. The magic inside me is purring softly, vibrating the center of my chest between my breasts. It would've reacted differently if I was in danger, right? I have to believe that.

I step closer to the old shifter taking the silver chalice with a shaking hand.

"Just a sip." He nods encouragingly and I want to scratch his eyes out.

"Don't do it, Francesca," my mother snarls writhing next to Silas to get away from him.

"It'll be fine, mother." Sounding a lot more confident than I feel, I lift the cup to my lips and tip it up, swallowing as fast as I can while trying not to breathe. "It's nothing bad," I murmur when nothing cataclysmic happens.

The chalice flips from my numb hand.

Dropping on my knees, my head snaps up and the loud-est, most tortured scream rattles the walls and windows of the academy. It's coming from me; I can feel my vocal cords shredding into ribbons and the inside of my throat bleeding, but I can't stop it. I'm melting from the inside. My body starts convulsing, all my limbs flailing while powers pump through my veins, burning everything in their path to ashes.

It lasts for many lifetimes, at least that's how it feels to me. When the pain finally stops, a cool breeze fills my body, mending everything that was ripped apart. My mind is clearing slowly and I almost weep knowing I never have to feel that again. That's when I begin screaming in my mind.

My arms push me up and I climb to my feet. The three Board members are watching me with rapt attention. I have no control of my movements and I'm well aware that the magic of the academy is in control. Whispers fill my head like a cloud of bees swarming closer and closer. Silas drops my mother and I watch dispassionately as she moves to the metal bed where my brother is laying covered with a sheet. It takes a second to realize she is placing herself between me and him because I'm walking toward my sibling.

Passing Silas, I snatch a dagger I didn't know he had from the small of his back. My mother lifts both arms to the side, making herself look bigger than she is in hopes to ward me off. I can feel the three Board members moving closer at my back. My soul is crying, begging the magic to release its hold and stop what I know is coming.

'No! Please no!' my mind screams and the buzzing stops just as I push my mother out of my way hard enough to send her flying to the end of the large dining hall.

"It is a mercy act, child." Many voices speaking at once fill my head. "You will be grateful when you find the truth that it was your hand to offer peace to the blood of your blood. In a war for power, this is not a sacrifice to weep about. I offer you a chance to avenge him."

I scream and claw inside my head but my body is calm

and not in my control. My arm lifts and slashes down, severing my brother's head, the blade passing through his neck like through butter. It falls off the bed and rolls out of sight, but the image of it is burned into my retinas. Tears run freely down my face, wetting the dried blood from my fight with Alexius. I numbly wonder if my brother's head joined his on the floor, but I don't look.

I can't look.

My mother's sobs are faint but they grow louder and she starts screaming at me, throwing every vile name under the moon my way. It's nothing less than I deserve. The dagger with the thick red blood dripping from it tumbles from my hand when my fingers go limp, cluttering on the floor.

Whatever soundproof barrier is placed around us pops like a bubble and everyone comes to life. The building is trembling from the fury coming from Zoltan when he pounces on Silas, but I can't find it in me to even let him see me like this. There is only one person I want to see right now. Only one person can help me do what I need to do.

Spinning on my heel, I run out of the hall faster than I've ever done before. Everyone is fighting in the dining hall so I'm lucky they don't notice I slip away. The halls blur around me and the door to my room crashes open, the hinges breaking, tilting it to one side. Like a whirl, I yank on sheets and drawers until I find what I am looking for and fly out of my room without a second's delay. In one way, it's good everyone else is occupied fighting the Board members. I don't want anyone coming with me right now. Out of the academy building, I bolt to the left straight at the open field where the portal swirls without a care in the world. If hunters are still gathered on the other side, even better. I will rip them apart limb from limb with my bare hands.

Not giving myself time to hesitate, I throw myself at the

portal head first. It spits me out on the other side with no side effects at all. Or I might be numb from the pain I already went through by giving the oath. I don't care. Dropping on my feet in the alley with its burning stench of the human realm, I place the coal in front of me and, sitting back on my haunches, I wait. She said she will come. I have to believe her.

Tenebris sails through the portal landing agile on his paws. He locks his gaze on mine for a moment before settling next to me. We sit in silence for what feels like forever. My heart sinks when a long enough time passes and she doesn't come. My lower lip is trembling, and I know the shock is wearing off. I need to be away from everyone and everything when that happens. No one is going to see me break. Not even the panther.

"Hello, cousin." Myst's husky voice reaches my ears from the mouth of the alley.

"We are nothing to each other." I sound toneless and hollow.

"Yet we share blood." Pushing off the wall, she moves closer eyeing the feline warily. "But that's not why you called me."

"I killed my brother," I blurt out past the lump in my throat.

"And you need a shoulder to cry on?" A look of disappointment crosses her delicate features.

"I have a serpentine stone that my father left me." that gets her attention more than anything else. "It's yours if you help me."

Locking my gaze with hers, I stare at her long enough that she starts shuffling her feet, the thin heels of her boots scraping the concrete.

"You have changed." Narrowing her eyes, she squints at

me. "Are you looking for me to feel sorry for you? What is it you want from me Francesca?"

"Revenge." The magic inside me sends a pulse through my entire body and Myst jerks back. "I'm going to kill them all."

"Now we are talking." She grins.

Next in the Daywalker Series

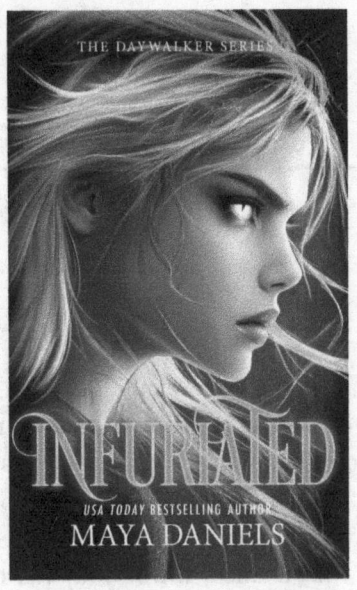

vinci-books.com/infuriated

No victory is worth the blood of the ones I love.

I woke the Dragon Blood—and I might already regret it. Soren's mercy is lethal, Zoltan's ready to burn the world, and me? I'm one breath from doing the same.

Turn the page for a free preview…

Infuriated: Chapter One

"Drake! Your ass better be awake!"

Jolted out of a fitful sleep by the shout, my legs scissor and tangle in the sheets. I kick something heavy, and it jerks away when I kick it. Whatever it is, it shifts to the left of the bed, the mattress dipping low enough to roll me to my side until I collide with a thick, warm body full of muscle. My mind is stuck between the weird dreams that have been on loop every night and the momentary panic knowing someone is inside my place, although I can't recall which place it is. An engine rumbles, picking up in volume somewhere outside. Seeing only darkness in front of my eyes, I blink owlishly to try to clear my vision.

The darkness shifts in my face.

With a shriek, I shove away from it, but I misjudge the strength I put behind my push and end up wind-milling my arms for a long second before I land hard on the floor, bruising my tailbone as my naked ass slaps on the parquet. The springs on the metal frame protest and squeak when a huge black head with piercing emerald eyes peeks down at me from the top of the bed. Tenebris smirks, and that stupid gaze of his travels over my naked body sprawled on the ground. In this moment, I realize it wasn't an engine that I heard. It was him purring next to me. He must have snuck in again in the middle of the night and crawled in beside me, and he had to have known I'd be angry about it the moment I woke up.

"Drake!"

The banging of cabinets and the tinkling of ceramic mugs comes from the kitchen down the hall, followed by too-loud grumbling and cursing. Ignoring the damn panther and the frustrated muttering of the intruder, my head moves slowly as I look around the room, my eyes stopping at the slightly-parted curtains on the window where a barely-there light from the approaching dawn is struggling to be seen. The sight of the familiar place I've called home in the last week slows the thundering in my chest and calms the magic pulsing with its own beat between my breasts, which allows me to finally take a full breath and release it slowly.

"Oh good, you're up." Tucking my legs under me, I jump to my feet and face Myst. "I was going to drag you out of bed by your feet."

She'll do it, too. As a matter of fact, she has done it twice so far. The second time she barely escaped Tenebris's teeth, which were an inch from her face. My eyes flick from her to the panther and he cocks his head to the side, his right ear swiveling like a satellite dish while he eyes Myst contemplatively. I wonder if he is thinking the same.

"Don't even think about it." Pulling the teaspoon out of her mouth—she went after the peanut butter again even though I hid the damn jar—Myst stabs the air with it, pointing it from the panther's face to mine. "I'll neuter him and stab you in the boob with this spoon before either of you move."

"Why are you here at this ungodly hour, Myst?" Jamming my fists on my hips, I glare at her as I try to ignore the fact that I'm butt naked and Tenebris is giving me side-eyed glances. "And have you heard of knocking? It's what normal people do instead of breaking into someone's home."

"We"—She twirls the spoon in the air between us, grinning like a fiend— "are neither normal people, nor is this your home. It's mine, and I let you stay here. And that brings me to the reason I'm here at this ungodly hour, as you so eloquently put it. He is getting to be the biggest pain in my ass, and I've had a lot of pains in my ass, trust me. It says a lot about the situation."

'What are you talking about?"

I can't help but wonder if the female is losing her mind. Myst always acts a little unhinged, which keeps anyone around her wary and on their toes. She is muttering under her breath even now as she scowls at her feet. I have a hard time figuring out what version is the real her and which one she uses to keep people away from her, to be honest. And they say I'm weird and unstable.

"I've managed to keep us hidden, even against the added efforts he has put into his search, but there's no denying the fact that he is pulling out the big guns. Looking at you like this, I can't say I blame him, but enough is enough." Her chocolate eyes lift to my face and darken to swirling shadows. Black mist covers the whites, and the effect curdles my blood. "If he sends that arrogant jerk my way, I'm going to slaughter you all." She blinks once and the darkness disappears like it was never there, the switch in her attitude almost giving me whiplash. A bright smile blossoms on her face. "You look like you need coffee, Chicca. Good thing I started the brewer. Hurry up and get dressed because we have things to do."

With that, she claps her hands happily, spins around, and vanishes in the hall leaving me staring at the empty doorway with my jaw hanging to my chest. Lifting my gaze to Tenebris, he looks as confused as I feel. He even shakes his head sharply while rubbing a plate-sized paw over his head twice, his tail twitching limply behind him.

"This is going to be a shitty day. I can feel it." I rub my forehead, releasing a heavy sigh that feels like it's torn all the way from my toes.

"We don't have all day!" Myst yells from the kitchen, the banging even louder than before. It makes me wonder if she's looking for something or if she's just making noise to piss me off.

Snatching the clothing that's draped over a chair in the corner of the bedroom, I stab my legs in the jeans angrily. Being around this female takes some getting used to. I'm not sure if it's just me, but her mood affects my emotions. She has a tendency to sweep in like a tornado, taking you on a wild ride that leaves you dazed when it ends.

Anger and rage have been a constant companion of mine since the Board knowingly—or unknowingly for that matter—forced me to kill my own brother. I didn't know the male, never knew I had a sibling even though I've seen him twice, though the second time he was unconscious with machines connected to his body. But he was mine. He was blood and they took him from me. What they did made them as bad as Roberti, if not worse, but either way they definitely earned a place on my shit list. My hatred for all of them burns in my veins day and night, but it gets overwhelming when Myst is in one of her moods. I can't think of anything but bloodlust … like right now.

Tugging a long-sleeved shirt over my head, I pad barefoot down the hall on silent feet. Tenebris is right on my heels, the heat of his body warming the back of my thighs even when I don't hear him move. Silent death I call him in my head. The panther is a sneaky little shit. Typical cat. An asshole like a cat, too.

"There you are." Myst plants a mug in my hands, wrapping my fingers around it and giving me a squeeze until she is sure I won't drop it. "Drink up."

Plopping on the high chair by the kitchen island, I lean my elbows on the counter and cradle the mug. The steam is fogging Myst's features even as it swirls under my nose like a siren song, so I blow on it before taking a sip. I'm not a big coffee drinker, preferring a good tea over the vile dirt water, but on days like this I welcome the kick it'll give me.

"Let's start from the beginning." Gingerly, I set the mug down before it burns the palms of my hands. The coffee is unsweetened and black like my soul … or maybe hers. It's a toss-up between the two of us, honestly. "Who pissed you off so much that you showed up here a couple of hours before you normally would?"

I don't like morning people. They are chirpy, bright-eyed, and bushy-tailed at hours that even the devil himself wants to dig a hole and hide. It's unnatural, especially for my kind. We are creatures of the night, Daywalkers included. We should never be bright-eyed or bushy-tailed … well, besides Tenebris, whose tail fluffs up in anger when he's ready to pounce.

"The powers are shifting. He will send the jerk to find

me next just so he can get to you." Leaning a hip on the island across from me, she folds her arms under her breasts. "It's not going to happen." Huffing in frustration, she glares at my coffee. "That's a low blow even for him."

"Who?" She jerks at my shout, but I can't help it. I'm at my wits end with her. "You might as well speak in a foreign language, Myst. I don't understand a word coming out of your mouth."

"Zoltan." Her voice is calm and flat.

My heart, on the other hand, jumps to the roof of my mouth, somersaulting between my throat and my chest before plummeting to my feet and splattering on the floor. Swaying on the chair, I grip the island tightly with my fingers so I don't fall off it, bright spots dancing at the edges of my vision. Tenebris chirps, bumping his head on my leg to get my attention. It is just what I need to pull me out of the panic threatening to suffocate me. Prying my fingers off the edge of the counter, which I'm clutching with a white-knuckled grip, I sink them into his fur and ground myself to his solid presence.

"We need to hide." Pushing the words through numb lips, my nostrils flare as I take control of my unsteady breathing.

I don't want to see Zoltan. Not now, and not until I have killed every single one of the ones who thought it'd be fun to play games with my life, every single one of them who thought they could take control of my actions to make me a puppet in their game. The vampire will want to take me back to the academy because in his head that's my home, so that's where I belong. He couldn't be more wrong, but I don't have the energy to explain it to him, nor do I want to.

"I will make sure he doesn't find you if that's what you want." Tilting her head to the side, Myst watches me with a knowing look. It's plain as day that she understands exactly how I feel, and I have a feeling Fenrir is the reason.

What a fucking mess.

"I don't want to see any of them." Swallowing thickly, I scrape my nails over Tenebris's head and shoulders, his purr growing louder by the second. "Not yet." Myst flicks her gaze to the panther, and when she turns to me again her eyebrow is cocked like an arrow. "If you showed up sooner, he wouldn't be here either. I had no choice but to let him come along."

"Sometimes, Chicca, I wonder if you believe the lies you tell everyone or if you're simply so naïve that think you are telling the truth."

"I don't need a therapist, Myst." Snatching the mug off the island, the hot liquid sloshes over my hand and burns my skin. I don't wipe it, instead relishing in the pain because it takes my mind off other things. Tightening my hold, I chug half of the scolding coffee, daring her to say a word by not looking away from her face. "I need to find Roberti and end this once and for all."

"Mhmm." Her eyes narrow slightly but she doesn't say anything, only lifts her own mug to her lips and sips the coffee as she watches me with her forehead scrunched in contemplation. "And you still need me for that because you are nowhere ready to walk among humans without bringing attention to yourself."

"I'm learning." I hate that I sound defensive because I'm more upset with myself than she'll ever be for taking this long to learn a simple parlor trick. "I'll try harder." When her lips twitch, my palm itches to slap her. "I'm paying you to help me."

"Which reminds me." Lowering her mug with a clunk, she regards me through a slanted gaze, suspicion oozing out of her every pore. "You promised a serpentine stone. One I have yet to see."

"I'm not lying to you. I have the stone; I just left it at a friend's place. You'll have it the moment I get it back. Trust me, I never go back on my word."

"You have a serpentine and you just leave it at a friend's place?" Her eyebrows almost disappear in her hairline. "Let's go back to my statement from earlier. I'm leaning more towards naïve right now."

"What's the big deal anyway?" Tossing back the remaining coffee, I slam the empty mug on the island. "It's a stupid rock."

Myst chokes on her tongue, and I swear Tenebris snickers.

"The damn thing almost killed me." Muttering under my breath, I jump off the chair.

"Say what now?" The sharp, intent look on her face chills me to the bone, and I regret not keeping my mouth shut.

"What's the plan?" Switching the subject, I stretch my arms above my head. I didn't sleep well at all. Again. Everything hurts and I'm more tired now than I was a few days ago.

Myst searches my face long enough to make me uncomfortable, so I shuffle my feet and force my hands to hang limply at my sides so I don't fidget. With effort, I keep my breathing even, pretending I don't notice how still Tenebris is next to me. Nothing living should be able to stay motionless like he does. Goosebumps pop up on my arms and legs.

"We continue practicing until it gets dark," she finally says, giving the panther a quick look. "Then we hunt for Roberti."

"Oh, joy!" My fake enthusiasm about practicing makes Myst grin.

I never want to see a chilling smile like that as long as I live.

Grab your copy…
vinci-books.com/infuriated

About the Author

Maya Daniels, USA Today Bestselling and multi-award-winning supernatural suspense author, is a fun-loving woman with many talents.

She traveled the world, gaining life experiences that helped her career as an investigative journalist, as well as her storytelling. Maya writes compelling tales of magic, mythical creatures, loyalty, and life-changing friendships with snarky female characters—much like herself.

Her travels have taken her to Europe, Africa, Asia, Australia, and America. Born with her feet in motion, she currently resides in Ohio, spinning her next epic story that you will not want to put down.

Her biggest 'sins' are her love of chocolate and coffee—through an IV drip! One to never sit still, Maya practices Reiki healing, different types of martial arts, reads about the arcane, talks to furry creatures more than humans, picks up a sledgehammer for home improvement, and travels with her fated mate, seeking her own adventures.